Max and Menna

Max and Menna

Shauna Kelley

Athens, Ohio

Max and Menna

Published by:
Lucky Press, LLC, PO Box 754, Athens, OH 45701-0754
Email: books@luckypress.com   SAN: 850-9697
Visit the publisher's website: www.LuckyPress.com
Visit the author's blog: mmshaunakelley.blogspot.com
Purchase order fax: 614-413-2820 email: sales@luckypress.com

Hardcover: ISBN: 978-0-9844627-3-5
Paperback: ISBN: 978-0-9844627-4-2
Library of Congress Control Number: 2010925471

Author's photograph by Sarah Kubel
Book Design by Janice Phelps, LLC

PRINTED IN THE UNITED STATES OF AMERICA

Max and Menna is a work of fiction and descriptions of events and characters are fictitious creations of the author's imagination.

Kelley, Shauna.
    Max and Menna / Shauna Kelley. — Athens, Ohio : Lucky Press, c2011.

        p. ; cm.

        ISBN: 978-0-9844627-3-5 (cloth) ; 978-0-9844627-4-2 (pbk.)

        1. Children of alcoholics—Fiction. 2. Twins—Fiction. 3. Brothers and sisters—Fiction. 4. Friendship—Fiction. 5. Teenagers—Alabama—Fiction. 6. Bildungsromans. I. Title.

PS3611.E4437 M39 2011   2010925471
813.6--dc22   1011

To my mother, with hopes that she knows that
at the end of my days, success will not be measured
by any possession, or any accomplishment,
but by whether or not I was able to ever be
half the woman that she is.

Acknowledgments

With great thanks to those who have helped me find my voice as a writer. First and foremost, this means Madison Smart Bell, whose patience in reading early drafts of this work (many of them just plain terrible) was absolutely invaluable. Also to many other writers who encouraged me throughout the way, including Susan Shreve, Todd Jackson, and Geoff Becker.

I also must thank my parents and my grandfather, who avoided expressing their concern as they mailed check after check to pay for a degree in creative writing. I will leave it to my readers to decide if their money was wasted.

I greatly appreciate the constructive, yet honest feedback of Sarah Kubel, my very best friend, who read the first draft and answered countless questions with patience and good ideas. I must thank her, as well, for always knowing the right encouraging words and understanding my babble more often than anyone else.

I am also grateful to Kendrick Wilson, who remembers all of the nice things people have said about my writing, even if I don't.

And finally, to those great writers whose works move me and inspire me and show me how beautiful a story can be, which include Margaret Atwood, John Irving, and Sherman Alexie. I aim to keep writing and keep reading and maybe one day exhibit the talent you all show so gracefully.

Chapter One

*H*e is awake. He lies very still, knowing that the slightest movement will betray his awareness, and he is too happy to watch her.

She is sitting in the chair across the room, her back to him, scribbling away in her journal. Her back, smooth and naked, arcs forward, twists ever so slightly to the side. The room is scantly lit, but it seems that every ounce of illumination is drawn to her, catches her, glistens off of the beads of sweat that have collected on her dark brown skin.

The heat is stifling. The windows are all open, but serve only to allow more of the stillness from outside to permeate the air within, air that feels thick and heavy.

He smiles to himself, noticing the way her neck curves away from her shoulders, how wisps of her thick, black hair escape from the sloppy knot on top of her head and topple down about her. He smiles, notices the time on the clock beside him, and sits up, suddenly sullen.

In an instant she has turned to face him. They stare at each other in silence for a moment. Then she sighs. "I guess you're leaving now."

He looks down from her face, to the plain of her chest, the swelling of her exposed breasts, the curves of her stomach. "You know why I have to."

She gets up from the chair, walks to the bed and sits on the side, her back to him, looking out the open window. Beyond the curtains are several more ramshackle homes. They are small, like dog houses in the distance, all equally assaulted by the heat. "I know why you think you have to."

He sits on the opposite side of the bed, their backs now to each other. There is friction in the air between them. "I don't know how she found me," he muses to himself. "I thought I was impossible to find."

"I found you once, too," she reminds him. "I thought for good."

He stands, turns to stare at the blankness of her back. "You did," he says. "I will come back."

She twists about to look at him. "No one leaves here and comes back willingly."

"I came here willingly," he says.

"Once," she says. "Only once."

"I will come back."

"I don't believe that."

"Then come with me," he says.

Silence. These words are foreign coming from him, as is anything indicating how he felt about her. She thinks, imagines what it will be like in the world far from here. "I can't." She gets up and heads out of the room. He watches her as she goes, following the rippling of her muscles under taut skin as she walks, then gets up and begins to pack.

She returns several minutes later with something in her hand. The darkness hides it from him, but before long, he hears ice clinking against glass, the sound of her taking a long, burning sip, and an intense wave of sadness rolls over him.

"Will you still be here when I get back?"

"I'm not your mother, Max," she says, "and I'm not them." She nods at the window, indicating the houses beyond hers. "I'm not you."

"I know that," he echoes. And he does.

He clicks the suitcase closed and she shutters. He walks to her, leans over her and whispers. "Please tell me you understand why I have to go."

"I can't," she retorts quickly. "If you had told me about her yesterday, or last week, maybe. But you never told me anything."

He looks at the floor, sadness in his eyes, and then looks back to her. "I'll make you understand."

He leaves the room, and she sighs, fighting tears and thinking it's for good. Then she turns, sees the suitcase closed on the bed, and sobs quietly. Her silence returns when he does, his hands full of papers.

She recognizes them at once, remembers so many hours of him sitting, bent over his typewriter and banging away, remembers all the times he averted her questions with kisses, all the times he shoved them in a drawer as she approached. She had never asked to see these papers, had somehow known they would be forbidden. And now he hands them to her, and they slide into her hands easily. She feels, instantly, that something has changed. Something between them has fallen.

She takes them, pulls them into her lap, and curls around them. He watches her, a look of near-desperation playing on his face, and then turns from her.

"Take something," she says, and then pulls in a long, deep breath to steady her nerves.

"What?" he asks.

"Take something of mine, anything, but take something of me with you," she says.

"I don't need something of yours to remember you, Netis. I won't be gone that long," he says. He also inhales, hoping she doesn't notice a redness around his eyes, brought on by exhaustion, and worry, and frustration at how big a deal she is making of this

3

trip. This is also from a welling terror that perhaps she can see something coming that he cannot.

"I know that, but I want you to take something anyway," she says. "Pull something out of that top drawer."

He opens her bureau, and looks at a scattered display of objects. From amidst a necklace, three bottle caps, a stack of old photos, and two half-burnt candles, he pulls out a small knife in a leather sheath.

"Interesting choice," she says.

He smiles sardonically. "It travels well."

"Good-bye," she says, with more finality than she intends.

He retrieves his suitcase, kisses her on the shoulder, and stops at the door. "I will be back."

She resists looking at him. "You'll be out of the county by sunrise, and I will never see you again."

Wordlessly, he closes the door behind him. The voice that hangs in the air is neither his nor hers, but the echoes reverberated through the phone. She had heard them clearly when he picked up the receiver late last night. "Max, my brother, I need you."

Brother. Part of the life of a sister she never knew he had, another piece of a life he had always kept so carefully hidden.

In the wake of his absence she sheds a few tears. They mingle with her perspiration, the tense and abusive air; the whole room begins to swim about her. She finishes her drink in one gulp, feeling it burn, gagging slightly. She wonders if she should have another, then remembers how this was the last of the bottle she had to dust before opening.

The first paper in the pile sticks to her as she straightens out to read. She peels it from her skin and glances at it. In the darkness the words are only shadows on the page. She sets the whole pile on the desk, on top of her journal, and switches on the light.

My mother told me once, her speech slurred and eyes glassy, that my father was a first class son of a bitch. I think I was seven, and from that day to this, those fuzzy, angry words are the only information I know about the other half of my parentage. And as for the half I lived with, my mother, well she was only half-alive to begin with.

But I guess that isn't the most essential information about my childhood. I don't really know what is. I had hoped since I left home that childhood itself wasn't essential, that I could easily walk away from it and bury it in the back of my mind.

I can't.

I was the man of the house, always. For as long as I remember, I always felt that it was my role, my job to protect them—my sisters—but mostly just one of them. I still can't bury it, can't leave it, can't forget them, but mostly her. She is part of me, quite literally I guess. I mean Menna, of course, my twin.

Netis stops, her eyes tripping over the end of the first page. Suddenly the strange, sad voice on the other end of the phone last night had a name.

The sun began to infiltrate, spreading strange shadows across her face. She glances out the window to the houses beyond, which seem very small and faint in the coming light. A chill spreads across her body in the stifling room. She turns over the first page, lays it on the desk, and turns back to reading.

Max

An Alabama summer is like a wet, wool blanket in the sweltering heat. The very air is thick, and scratchy, and no matter what you do you can't shake it from you. Everybody sweats, nobody really talks about it, and the days pass slowly, as if extending the torturous summer season just to spite all the little people slinking along, never above a slow walk, for the air just won't permit speed.

Perhaps that small corner of Alabama won't permit speed. It always feels to be a day, a week, a year behind the rest of the world. At least that's the way I always felt while I was growing up there. Granted, I didn't have the most ideal childhood, which could have quite possibly tainted my memories of the place.

But no, no that can't quite be it. At the time, I never minded the heat. I never minded the slow pace. I never minded the archaic opinions. At least not at first I didn't, not when I was younger. Then I didn't much notice, I guess. I didn't notice much at all, or worry about much. Just where Menna and I would play on a given day, and where our dinner would come from that night.

I can't think of Menna without thinking of our hill; well at least "our" hill when we were young. I guess all things change as you get older. I remember the day we found it. The day woke me early, dripping in through the curtains of the attic where we slept. I rolled over to see Menna, curled up on the floor beneath the window. The sun draped around her, spilling over her face, shining in her coal black hair.

It was early in the morning, and already the air was brutally moist.

She had kicked off the blankets in the night and now slept on the bare floor, her chin nearly resting on her knees. Her eyes were closed softly, resisting the tendrils of hair that fell into them. Her round cheeks were smudged with dirt from the floor, beads of sweat bursting forth and protesting the heat.

"Menna," I whispered, watching her eyes flutter open. It was nearly like looking in a mirror, my own dark brown eyes finding hers across the room.

A crash from below startled her. She sat straight up, soon finding herself listening to my mother scream from below. "God damn you Lily, I won't have this," she yelled, her voice high, scratchy and filling the attic.

"I don't give a damn what you'll have," Lily shrieked back. The door slammed, and I knew by the muttering that followed it must have been my older sister and not my mother that left because of this fight. My mother always muttered to herself when she was alone.

Menna glanced over at me and smiled in a sad sort of way. We were used to this argument, more dependable then an alarm clock, to wake us up. It had every day so far that summer, the summer after third grade. Menna and I were eight, mirror copies of each

6

other save for her hair being long and mine being short. In those days boys didn't have long hair.

Our eyes met, and I instantly knew what she was thinking—*out*—it was our way—subtle mind reading.

"You ready?" she whispered.

"Mom's at it already," I replied, knowing it was early, but still sure that she had been drinking. That vodka, that gin, that rum. She didn't have a favorite. Mom loved them all like children, and she consumed them all equally, and eagerly.

"Then let's get out of here," Menna suggested, walking by me and heading quietly down the stairs.

I followed. We had both slept in our clothes and so did not need to change, and it wouldn't have occurred to either of us to stop and brush our teeth, our hair, wash our faces, or bathe. Such things just weren't part of our ritual, and our mother didn't seem to care. Lily did, but only during the school year. Then she would make us wash in the morning, for she walked us to school and wouldn't be seen with any "grungy punks" from our side of town. Menna and I didn't pay much attention to how grungy we were or weren't, but when Lily spoke we listened.

My mom was on the couch when we peered around the corner from the second level. She was lying very still, her eyes closed, her hand wrapped firmly around a glass. Menna looked at me with a quick, uncertain stare. "Do we go?" she mouthed, wondering if it would be safe to pass my mother.

I shrugged, looked across the living room to notice that the front door was open. I nodded to it, and we both traced the distance of the room with our eyes. Maybe ten feet, but twenty steps for our little feet. Twenty very dangerous steps.

Finally Menna leaned over and pinched me softly. I glanced back at her, then down to my mother, who seemed to have fallen asleep. I stared for a few seconds, and then began to creep down the stairs. Menna followed, our bare feet making little noise on the rough, wooden steps. We hit the bottom and rounded the corner into the living room silently, then broke into an all out run for the door.

As we stepped outside I turned my head to notice that my mother had opened her eyes and was watching us go. I didn't stop running until we were at the end of the street. There was a small cul-de-sac there, with a wide-open field at the end. We threw ourselves into the grass at the end of the road and giggled with the elation that always followed getting out of the house.

I was on my back heaving and gasping for breath for a long time, Menna beside me doing the same. The sky was very clear that day, barely any clouds at all, and the sun had already begun to beat down on us. The heat made breathing hard. After a while Menna rolled up onto her side to stare at me. "We going to stay here all day?" she asked.

"I could," I replied, realizing how good it felt to be still and breath freely.

"You're boring," she said, and began to pound her feet angrily into the grass. The ground reverberated with the rhythmic *thump thump*.

"Quit it," I said quickly. The noise was irritating me.

"Don't you want to go somewhere?" she asked, her voice growing high and whiney.

"Menna, where do you want to go?" I asked, growing more and more angry at her inability to sit still.

"Anywhere but here," she said, and stood. Anywhere but here.

The field was lined at the far side with a row of trees. The big kids in the boys' room at school had told me they were haunted. I didn't think much of it at the time, thinking this was the typical kind of thing the big boys in the bathroom talked about. Girls and haunted woods—both ridiculous to me. Menna now stood and faced the forest, one ridiculous creation to another. "Let's go into them woods," she said.

"Into the woods?"

"Yeah," she said. "We've never been there before."

And she was right. Normally from the field we would head down to the creek on the other end of town where the big houses were. We would swim until one of the grown-ups came and yelled at us to get out of the water. Some of them were even bold enough to tell us to go to the reservation where we belonged. "We ain't Indians!" Menna would scream back at them, her voice angry, though I don't think she knew what was bad about being Indian in our town, just knew that it was bad. Then again, being us in our town was pretty damn bad as well but I didn't know that until much later.

There really wasn't a "reservation," exactly. There was a long fence and several families of Indians that lived on the other side. When schools were segregated, they went with the blacks. When the schools had integrated, they appeared, a handful of them, in classes with everyone else.

By the time Menna and I started school, most of the Indian children were so much older than us. Most of them had stopped coming to school anyway, and those that did, three or four of them, were in the high school, or at least many grades higher than we were.

Once we walked over to the fence of the reservation and stared in. Every now and then we would see some older kids playing in the dust and dirt, their clothes torn and dirty like ours. But the kids would never come talk to us, so we only ever walked to the fence that one time.

Mostly, on days like this, we would walk all the way through town to the school where there was a playground, but lately Menna didn't much like going through town. She said something about people looking at us funny there. I told her she sounded like Lily and she punched me in the shoulder. I'd hit her back even though her little girl fist hadn't hurt at all, mostly because I couldn't let no damn girl punch me around like that. I hit her partly, though I'm sure she didn't know it, because she had already picked up on something that I had not.

I stood beside her then, that day, staring at the woods, which suddenly looked so very far away. In our tiny town, this was the one place we had not probed. They seemed foreboding, ominous, and yet still mysterious, different, promising. Though I would never have said it to her, I didn't want to enter to find that those woods were just like everything else—small, staunch and exclusive.

9

I wonder now, did a seven-year-old think these thoughts? Had I yet figured out, then, how everyone looked at us? About the parties, the restaurants, and the conversations we were categorically left out of? Can I look back without everything that happened coloring my vision, clouding the place with a quiet disgust? I don't remember what I thought that day, I simply recall being terrified at the idea of entering the woods.

"It's just a bunch of trees," I said.

"So?" she said. "You're afraid of them ghosts."

"Am not."

"Are too."

"Am not."

"Then let's go." She had her chin pushed out in a sharp, defiant arc, and was staring at me with her arms crossed angrily across her chest. "Unless you're a 'fraidy cat."

"I ain't no 'fraidy cat," I spat back, taking off across the field. I knew this is exactly what she had wanted me to do, and the frustration that she had won the brewing argument before it started propelled me faster.

"Max, wait!" she called from behind. Though our bodies looked the same, mine was built faster and I used to delight in leaving Menna behind. I didn't wait this time, but reached the woods and plowed angrily into them, my head down to protect my face from the few branches that dared stoop low enough to attack a boy.

I could hear Menna tearing through the brush behind me, calling my name all the time, her voice going from angry to confused to scared. Finally she began to shriek my name. I turned to see if I could find her, but she was nowhere to be seen. My cheeks flushed, and my stomach quickly knotted with worry. If I had lost her, and these huge, foreboding woods had her . . .

"Menna?" I called, wheeling around and around, but not seeing her anywhere.

"Max!" she called back. I took a few steps in what I thought was the direction from where her voice had come, but tripped and fell before I made much progress. A rock on the ground tore into my leg, leaving a large and nasty gash as proof of my clumsiness. I leaned against a tree and examined the cut as the sound of Menna getting closer to me reached my ears. I called her name again, hearing her approach, and suddenly she was beside me.

"You dummy," she said, sitting down beside me and using the hem of her shirt to wipe the blood that was trickling down my leg. "That's what you get," she scolded. I recognized the tone in her voice as that of the ladies who yelled at us to get out of the creek, and who muttered about us under their breath as we walked through town.

"If you wouldn't have gotten lost . . . " I pointed out, my voice angry, but she could see the relief in my eyes, and I knew that she had won this little battle.

"You ran off without me," she said, sitting back on her heels and staring at my quizzically. Her hair fell about her face in a tangled mess. "And now we're lost."

"We ain't lost," I spat, standing and ignoring the stinging in my leg. "We're going that way," I said, pointing off through the woods.

"That's the way we *came* from," she said. "We go *that* way." And she took off walking in the opposite direction, not even waiting for me to respond. I felt the urge to hit her well within me, fed by my frustration at her stubbornness, but I did nothing but followed her sullenly, irritated that she had won another argument before it started.

The woods were fairly dark, though it was late morning by the time we really admitted we were lost. The trees had looked so small from the field, so thin, and now they were large and thick and every-where, obscuring the sun from us. My fear was tempered by a dark joy—we had found a place that was different. My breathing grew heavy and I was sure that the trees would steal the very air before it could reach us.

"Max," Menna said, turning to face me. I could see that she had begun to cry, "Max, I'm scared," she said. I looked at her face, her eyes, and saw that the simple statement didn't truly express her fear. She was terrified.

" 'Fraidy cat," I said. It was a mean thing to say, but I made my voice gentle and put my arm around her as I said it.

"I ain't no 'fraidy cat," she said, elbowing me, wiping the tears from her eyes and heading off to the left. I followed her again. After only a few moments we came across a rudimentary path. The trees had begun to attack it, spitting leaves and debris on the small area of clear dirt, sending their roots to create knots and swells. "See? And I found us a path," she said, smiling triumphantly as she negotiated her way onto the path and headed off farther into the woods.

I sighed and followed, knowing Menna to be stubborn and hardheaded most times. I guess I was too, I just didn't care as much about everything as she did. I would have been content to find my way out of the woods at that point and go to town, writing off the experience as a failure, and live with the knowledge that this big and different place existed.

Not Menna, though. She would not admit defeat and would not leave until our trip into the woods had found some purpose, until she had solved the mystery, though I'm not really sure what mystery that was. "Menna, where are we going?" I called up to her.

"Wherever this takes us," she replied, as though this was the most natural answer in the world. I shook my head and kept following until the path gave way abruptly to a small clearing. We stood at the fringes of the woods and stared up at a hill. Our hill.

The hill was surrounded by trees on all sides, rising from them like a castle. At the top of the hill was a small, run down swing set and what had once been a bench but was now only two stumps. The hill was grassy in large clumps, with patches of raw clay gleaming up like bald spots from it. Wildflowers spat up from the earth sporadically, giving the hill a patchwork look, rugged, and old. And halfway up sat a person. I thought it a girl at first, as I saw long black hair blowing in the wind behind a small, lithe body. Menna looked at the figure and charged ahead, her head high and haughty. "Menna!" I called after her, suddenly wary of the figure on the hill, but she kept plowing up the hill towards the person, so I followed, thinking I would protect her if need be, but knowing it was more than I didn't want to turn around and enter the woods without her.

We were almost to the small, huddled person when I realized that it wasn't a girl at all, but a boy. A boy with long, black hair. He looked probably to be a little older then us, and was most definitely Indian.

Everyone told us, teachers, parents, preachers, that Indians were, inextricably, bad and dangerous. This was the first one I had ever seen in person without the safe separation of a chain link fence.

"Menna," I said, grabbing her and holding her in place for a moment.

"What?" she reeled and faced me defiantly.

"He's an Indian," I said.

"What's wrong with that?" she demanded. I opened my mouth to answer her before realizing that I really didn't know. All I could think of were the disapproving faces of the women in our town, of the old silent movies our teachers showed where Indians killed and plundered, then laughed about it.

"He ain't going to talk to you," I said, and she just smiled like she knew a secret and kept right on charging up the hill.

"Hey," she called as soon as the figure came within yelling range.

He didn't move. He sat cross-legged with his eyes closed, leaning back into the grass on his arms. She walked up next to him and sat down. I stopped a few paces back, wondering if he had a horse somewhere nearby. I had never been this close to an Indian before, but all the ones I'd seen in books from the library had horses. I went to the library a lot during the school year, and had read almost every book. The entire room had only two books on Indians, and one said they were mean and blood-thirsty like pirates, and would take your women away if you let him. At this point in time I almost hoped he would take Menna, though I couldn't imagine why anyone would want to.

The other book in the library said Indians were poor and said prayers to trees and stuff. That had seemed so funny at the time, praying to trees and all. Almost as funny as wanting to take women. I lived with three of them, and as far as I was concerned, they were all up for grabs.

But this boy looked different, like a member of the ragged army we had seen through the fence. As I thought about it, I realized those kids didn't have horses. Nonetheless, I was convinced that somewhere, out of sight, this boy had one.

Menna didn't appear to be too concerned with the location of this boy's horse. She said, "Hey," again, and when he didn't respond she nudged him gently in the ribs.

The boy's face, still placid and unconcerned, turned slowly towards her. Then his eyes opened and he regarded her calmly before turning back to his original position.

"Menna, leave him alone, he doesn't want to talk to you," I informed her from my observing post several feet away.

"What's he doing?" she asked me, staring at him as though he had three eyes and a tail. To Menna, that might have been slightly less puzzling then someone who just didn't want to talk to her.

"He's probably praying," I told her.

"What for? It ain't Sunday," she pointed out.

"Indians don't pray to God," I told her, suddenly very proud of my knowledge of Indians. "They pray to rocks and bushes and trees and stuff."

Suddenly I noticed that the boy was smiling very broadly. Menna let out a dramatic and confused sigh and he erupted into laughter.

"What's he laughing at?" she asked me. I shrugged and she turned to face him, as though wondering if this burst of sound meant he would speak to her. "What you laughing at?"

"You," he said quite calmly, then reclined back into the grass, his belly still shaking with amusement.

I stared quietly at Menna for a moment, watching the way the anger swelled within her. Within seconds she had talked herself into indignancy at the gall of this boy, this *Indian* for laughing at her. Finally she smacked him squarely on the stomach. Her hand struck his flesh with a resounding *thwap*. He sat up instantly and looked at her, anger clouding his dark brown eyes.

14

"What do you think you're doing, little girl?"

"I'm hitting you," she replied, smacking him again, this time in the shoulder. "How dare you laugh at me. You're the one praying to stones."

He stared at her for a while, and I noticed how small she looked against him, her tiny body, tiny features, tiny understanding. After a full minute the smile returned to his face. "I wasn't praying to stones. I was thinking."

"With your eyes closed?" she demanded.

"Yes," he said. "I think best with my eyes closed."

"Oh," she said softly. "Why didn't you say so right off?"

"I needed to finish my thought."

Menna nodded, as though this made perfect sense, laid on her belly in the grass, dirty feet thrust in the air, and snuggled right up next to the boy. "I'm Menna," she said, "and that's my brother Max, and we're eight years old."

He smiled at me, then at her. "I'm Nick, I'm eleven."

"That doesn't sound like a very Indian name," Menna said.

"And what does sound like an Indian name?" he asked.

We both regarded this for a while before I blurted out "Pocahontas."

Again he laughed. "We don't have names like that. And we don't pray to stones."

"Then what do you do?" Menna asked. She seemed suddenly very interested in this boy.

"I do love the outdoors," he said, "I love it all, I just don't pray to it."

"That ain't what my teacher said."

"Your teacher is wrong," Nick said. We both met the comment with silence. Teachers were infallible to us. I mean, our mother certainly wasn't—for us, for kids our age, someone has to know everything to make the world work. And here he was, saying that just wasn't so.

After a while Nick got up to leave. Menna frowned and asked him to stay.

"I can't, I have to get back. I'm not supposed to be on this side of the fence."

"Why not?" we asked.

"I don't know." He looked far off into the trees, towards our house for a while. "My mom thinks it's dangerous out here."

Menna laughed. "Our mom thinks it's dangerous in there."

Nick smiled. "Maybe our moms should get together. Bring yours over sometime." We all laughed at the idea for a moment, before silence overtook us again.

"How big is it?" Menna asked. We knew little of what was on the other side of that fence. Our town had erected the fence to separate us from the reservation many years before, and we never saw the other side, except through strained glances, fingers gripping chain link.

"Sometimes," he said, "it seems like the whole world is inside of it. Other times, it seems that you can't sigh without ruffling someone's hair."

He didn't say good-bye, just turned and walked away. We, of course, did not understand what he had just said at all, but sat in silence thinking about it anyway. I moved beside my sister and we mused together.

The day had grown into something truly amazing. It was one of those June days when the sun seemed to melt from the sky like butter, dripping down onto everything, spreading lethargy. This was the perfect day to lie on a grassy hill and just think.

It must have been an hour later when Menna finally nudged me with her foot. "He talks like a grown-up," she said. I nodded in agreement, his words still rolling around my befuddled head, refusing to join together in some coherent order. "And he doesn't seem so bad."

And he didn't. He talked like a grown-up, but had been nice to us, like a kid might be if the grown-ups didn't make them stay away from us. That had always made me angry before, but on that day, as I thought about it, I smiled a bit with the realization that grown-ups made kids stay away from Indians too.

After another long period of silence Menna turned to look me squarely in the face. "Why is being an Indian so bad?"

I often asked myself this question. One of the books I had read about them made them seem so harmless, but that couldn't be true. The way the adults spat that word at us when they told us to go away, the way people walked by the fence with their eyes straight ahead as though afraid to look on the other side, the way the teachers in school never would talk about that fence and the inhabitants it kept decisively away from us—all of these things meant something bad. And yet, nobody ever said what.

"I don't know," I said. "We should ask Lily."

To us, our older sister was the resident expert on every question we might have. She usually regarded us with nothing but disdain, but on some days when she and Mom didn't fight, she would answer our questions, sometimes even smile.

"We should," Menna agreed emphatically.

Menna

When Max and I were younger we lived in a little town surrounded by a very big desert. Well, it wasn't really a desert, but it was nothingness in the form of red clay fields and magnolia trees. We were drenched in heat, like in the desert, and we could not wander very far, as though the sands would trap us. West of town there was a fence, and on the other side of the fence were Indians. We didn't speak to them, we rarely spoke of them. There weren't any kids our age over there, and the older kids went to the high school like the kids from our town did, but they did so with a silence surrounding them. It was small, that village on the other side of the fence, but to me it seemed endless, mysterious, wide, vast—anything that could pique a child's interest was embodied in the world just beyond rusted chain link.

Then I met Nick.

The more I talked to Nick, the more and more that world shrank and shrank until it seemed as small and suffocating as our own little town.

Nick and I first met on my hill. Our hill. Max was with us, and the hill was his then too. That first day Nick laughed at me and made me angry and I made a vow to hate him for life. I didn't tell him, of course, or Max either. I was eight then, and just beginning to realize that while Max shared my face, my room, my life, he couldn't completely share *me*, and he wouldn't understand what about Nick's laugh had angered me so much.

And then I listened to Nick talk, heard him say strange, incomprehensible things. He said them so simply, so painfully simply, that I could not help but believe. He didn't seem as bad as everyone said Indians were. Nonetheless, I still vowed to hate him.

But the next day we went back to the hill.

"What are we doing here, *again*?" Max complained as we hiked through the woods. He was sweating, the heat around us felt like a cloak. The air was so humid I sometimes thought I could open my mouth and swallow to fight my thirst.

I ignored him, concentrating on where we were going. I had paid special attention the day before to the way we got home, but that night a conversation with my older sister Lily had filled my mind with so many other things that I couldn't seem to remember anything else.

"Indians are bad because they are savages," she had said simply after recovering from the shock of such a question. Lily was the knower-of-all as far as we were concerned, and the only grown-up who talked to us aside from our teachers. She wasn't actually a grown up, but as close as we could come in the months between school. I knew that she even had a picture of my father somewhere far back in her mind. I wanted that picture, but knew it was something she would never share with me.

"Oh," I said quietly, wanting her to believe that I understood her explanation. Then, I always wanted Lily to think I was her equal, and did little to make myself seem ignorant in her presence. Max, however, always with his questions, just wouldn't let it go.

"What's a savage?" he asked almost instantly. I elbowed him in the ribs and he flicked my arm where Lily couldn't see.

"A savage is someone who rapes women and steals things and dances naked around fires," she said. She was in one of her good moods that night. Other times she could be quite crabby, mean even.

"Why would they do that?" Max asked. He never did know when to keep his mouth shut.

Lily's face clouded with aggravation. "They just do!"

Though I could tell Max was still curious, still teeming with questions, he let that go. We had learned far earlier to read my sister's mood, and he was teetering on the edge of a bad one.

Her words, so harsh, troubled me, as we walked through the woods again. I had an image of Nick, naked, well as naked as I could imagine a boy at that time, dancing around a fire and howling at the moon. It was frightening and strange, and so far from how he had seemed the day before. I had to go see him again, to figure out what image was true, to figure out if Lily was right. I prayed he'd be there, and prayed that he hadn't transformed over night into a savage, as though her words could will it.

The trees around us seemed less formidable that day, more familiar, but we still got slightly lost on the way to the hill. We were both sticky with sweat when we arrived, the air clinging to us. We stood in the clearing at the bottom and noticed that, again, Nick sat about halfway up, again leaning back on his elbows with his eyes closed.

Max grabbed my arm as if to convince me that we shouldn't bother him, but I shrugged him off and headed defiantly towards Nick, suddenly emboldened by his stillness, which I took as evidence that Lily was wrong about him.

Nick didn't move as I charged up the hill and planted myself beside him. His lack of movement, and the hurt from his mockery the day before, suddenly filled me with a desire to very obviously ignore him.

And yet, the longer we sat in silence the more I began to realize that ignoring someone isn't fun if they ignore you back. Max stood several paces down from us, dramatically crossing and uncrossing his arms to demonstrate his annoyance. Finally he looked up at me and ordered me to say something.

My cheeks flushed—I was instantly furious with him. I opened my mouth to respond to him—to yell, scream, something to show my anger, but Nick beat me to it.

"She doesn't have to if she doesn't want to," he told Max.

Max looked at both of us and shrugged noncommittally before turning to sit with his back towards us.

The silence continued on for quite some time, though Nick's defense of me began to cool my anger at my brother, and quiet my desire to ignore him. After a little while I leaned to him and said, "So what's it like over there?"

"Over where?" he asked.

"The reservation," I said.

"You know it isn't really a reservation, right?" he said. His voice was sort of curt, but he then softened, and added, "It's just a bunch of us that live near each other. There are only about thirty of us."

"So what's that like?" Max asked.

He thought for a moment, for so long a moment I thought he was going to forget to answer me. Finally he simply said, "For me, it is sad."

At the time I was confused, but I know now, looking back, it was all he could say. It was probably the only word he knew to describe his life over there. "Why don't you leave?" I asked him.

"Because I can't," he said.

"Why?" I couldn't wrap my mind around these things.

"Where would I go if I left?"

Max jumped in with the next question. "Over here, on the other side of the fence?"

"And then what? People here would still know I belong there." He gestured towards his long hair, his dark skin. "I can't get away from that."

The words fell heavily down upon us. I sat, digesting them, studying his profile. His jaw line was sharp, pronounced, his nose broad, his eyes like darkness. And something about him was tremendously sad.

"Do you want leave?" Max asked, finally.

"More than anything," Nick said without hesitation. "I just want to take my cousin Molly and get out of there. I think things would be much better over here."

Max was looking at the ground quietly. "It ain't always so good over here."

"Well, not *here*, but just somewhere else. Somewhere far away," he said.

"Have you ever been outside of here?" I asked.

"Went down to Mobile once," he said. "Wasn't so much different from here."

"You like your cousin?" Max asked.

"Yes," he said. "She and I are good friends."

"We don't have cousins," Max said. "We don't really have nobody."

Nick looked up at him, saw the look on his face, turned to me, saw it reflected on mine, but said nothing. After a long time I couldn't take the silence. I flopped over onto my stomach and began asking him questions.

"What's your favorite color?"

"I don't know," he said, "never really thought about it."

"Ah, mine's yellow, because the sun is yellow, and I like the sun. I like being outside better than being inside."

Max sighed, but Nick smiled. "Me too."

"It's boring inside, don't you think?" I asked. To me "inside" meant home, or school, both of which were boring.

"Yes," Nick said.

"Do you go to school?" I asked.

"Of course he goes to school, dummy," Max spat.

"Yes, I go to school," Nick said, preventing the fight that was about to erupt. "I don't like it much, though."

"Me neither," I replied. "Max likes school, though. He likes it a lot. He reads all the time. Even the dictionary sometimes."

"You read the dictionary?" Nick asked him, smiling broadly.

"It's the only book we have in our house. When I finish a book after the library closes, I read the dictionary and learn new words," Max explained. He was always a bit touchy about the subject.

"Max is real smart," I told Nick.

"Am not," Max spat at me, poking me.

"Are too," I retorted. "You're smarter than I am."

Max accepted this with silence. He liked hearing me admit that he was better at something than I was. He was smarter than I was, though. I couldn't make myself read like he could. I couldn't read inside, the words always blurred together as my restlessness grew, and I ached to be outside. I couldn't read outside because I would rather be running instead.

Nick seemed to be thinking over our words. He sat very still and only occasionally glanced between the two of us. The quiet began to bother me, like an itch I was trying not to scratch. My restraint didn't last long. Finally, I blurted out my favorite question: "Do you have a father?"

"Menna!" Max turned to me, his face full of worry.

"What? I just want to know if he has a dad," I explained.

"Everyone has a dad," Nick said, again his quiet voice disrupting the brewing argument.

"We don't," I told him. "Just our mom."

"You have a dad," Nick told me, "you just don't know who he is."

The words sounded strange. I looked into Max's face, imagined us having a father, of "Father" being more than a vague concept and source of drunken muttering. The thought seemed very odd, like the word didn't fit us. It was too big, somehow, like Lily's hand-me-down jeans that slid from my hips when I walked.

"Do you live with your dad?" Max asked, turning halfway to watch Nick out of the corner of his eye.

"Yes, I live with both of my parents, my brother, my sister, my aunt, and my cousin," he said.

"We just live with our mom and our sister," Max told him.

"Our mom is crazy," I said. "She's all right sometimes, but then she drinks and it makes her crazy."

Nick smiled softly in a despondent kind of way. "That's what liquor does to you," he said. "I know lots of people who drink like that, but I never will. I hate that stuff."

"Me too," Max said, sitting down with his back to us.

"My mom and my older sister Lily fight all the time. Lily's like Mom, sometimes she's all right, sometimes she's not, but she don't drink the . . . " I paused and pronounced very slowly "l . . . iiii . . . ckk . . . er..."

Nick laughed, as did Max. My pride was hurt again, so I stopped talking and watched the trees. I felt then like I needed to be cautious about what I said around Nick for fear that I should again make myself the source of laughter.

The three of us sat for a very long time, just listening to nothing, thinking everything it seemed, wondering what, if anything to say. The silence, the expression on Nick's face, the assurance of the existence of my father, all of it suddenly made me feel an overwhelming sorrow, which only grew with each quiet moment that passed. As the sun began to sink back behind the hill, and our house began to beckon, the grumbling in our stomachs became audible, and I put my head down on the soft grass and cried quietly to myself. Max still had his back to me, and couldn't see, but Nick could.

He put his hand on my shoulder, gingerly at first, as though I might hit him, but then solidly. He pushed the hair from my face, met my eyes, and smiled softly in a way that made me feel like I could stop crying.

"I should get home," Nick said suddenly, standing and waving to us.

"Bye," we called as he walked away.

"He's alluring," Max said.

"Max, don't use none of your smart words on me," I said, punching him in the shoulder.

"I like him," Max simplified. I agreed and we headed home.

This, our fourth trip through the woods, was uneventful. We had begun to learn where to go, this dead branch meaning veer left, this oak tree meaning straight ahead.

Our mother was asleep on the couch as we tiptoed in. Max approached her, noticed an empty bottle by her feet. Her mouth was open, a tiny puddle of saliva forming on the pillow below her head. Max brushed her hair out of her face, and covered her with a blanket. He did this kind of thing often when she was passed out. I sometimes wonder now if she even realized it when she woke up.

Lily was sitting in the kitchen, staring off into nothing. We walked past her to the cabinets and found an open box of cereal. My hunger had grown to the point of nausea.

"Have either of you eaten all day?" Lily asked.

We both looked up at her, surprised by the question. We both instantly noticed the swollen, black eye that decorated her face.

"Lily, you OK?" Max asked.

"Fine," she said fiercely, and Max knew then to drop it.

"No, we ain't eaten," I answered.

"OK," she said, getting up. She found our mother's purse, reached inside, pulled out some money and bid us to follow.

"Lily, Mom ain't going to like you digging in her purse," Max said as we followed her outside and down the steps.

"Mom ain't going to notice. Besides, she missed work again today. She's bound to get fired soon and we might as well take advantage of the money while she has it."

I can't imagine now, looking back, how my mother paid for us to have a house, much less occasionally put food in it. She held many jobs, but never for more then three or four months.

We walked through town to a small diner on the north side, far away from our house and the fence. We walked in and waited to be seated. After a long time the hostess walked over and informed us that she didn't want any trouble.

"Neither do we," Lily said. "We just want to eat." Her voice was ice.

The woman, obviously unhappy at the response, picked up three menus from the counter and walked away, perhaps expecting us to follow. Eventually we did, finding ourselves sitting at a small, dirty table in the back.

I couldn't remember having ever been out to eat before, and I wasn't sure how to behave, so I watched Lily and mimicked her. She opened her menu and poured over it, as if thinking very hard. I opened mine and looked at the pictures, unable to read many of the words.

The waitress came over and stood idly by, until Lily looked up and ordered us all sodas. The waitress walked away.

"Menna," Lily said, "do you want a cheeseburger or grilled cheese?"

"Grilled cheese," I said quietly.

"Max?"

"Cheeseburger."

Lily told the waitress when she came back, handed her our menus and sat quietly with her arms folded on the table.

"Have you ever been here before?" Max asked.

"Yes," she said. "Emery brought me once."

"Who's Emery?"

"You ask a lot of questions, Max," she said quietly, signaling that the conversation was over.

We ate in silence, Max and I, a bit bewildered by our surroundings, Lily sullenly mute. Lily paid the check with the crumpled bill she had taken from our mother, then ushered us quickly out.

"Why did we come all the way over there?" Max asked on the way home, as we passed by another restaurant.

"I like that place," she said quietly. "It's far from home."

I heard the defeat in her voice, and it exacerbated the sadness I had known all day. "Lily," I said, a question nagging me, a question that I feared to ask, "you don't like being home much do you?"

She looked at me as though I was alien, as though she had never seen me before. Finally, "No, Menna, I really don't like it there."

"Why don't you leave?" Max asked.

She sighed, "I'm fourteen, where would I go?"

Mom was still sound asleep when we walked back in, still in the exact same position, the saliva forming a large wet spot on her pillow. She was snoring slightly, and the room was now rich with the acrid odor of her urine, which saturated the couch, dripped down and formed a small puddle on the floor beneath her.

"Oh, God," Lily said, covering her nose and heading back into her bedroom. Max and I stood in the doorway and stared, before Max sighed softly and went to find a clean towel.

He cleaned up the mess wordlessly while I stood and watched, feeling oddly out of place in my own body.

When the floor was spotless, Max walked quietly up to the attic and I followed.

I'm sure he was already crying by the time I entered the room, but he did his best to conceal it. I knelt and wrapped my arms around him.

There were so many nights like these when all we had were each other.

Chapter Two

*M*enn . . . stop . . . " Cole says quietly from the passenger seat. Only then does Menna realize that the girl is no longer napping, probably awakened by the anxious tapping on the steering wheel. She quiets her hand by grasping the leather hard until her knuckles show white through the skin.

"Sorry, honey, forgot I was doing it," she explains, noting that Cole merely nods and rolls over to return to sleeping.

She glances at the clock— 4:13 AM and still nothing in sight but trucks. Her eyes have begun to ache, feeling gritty from sleep's attempts to take over. She blinks hard, and then rolls the window down a crack, letting the dry, crisp air into the car. Cole sighs audibly and sits up.

"If you needed me to keep you awake, why didn't you just say so?"

Menna turns to her and smiles. "I didn't realize till just now how tired I am, I was lost in thought."

"Oh," Cole says, rolling down her window and dangling her feet out the side of the car. "Do you miss living down here?"

Menna looks at her for several seconds, her eyes fully away from the road, which doesn't seem to matter. The road doesn't move. Then she smiles a soft sad smile and merely says, "Yes."

There is silence for a few more minutes, then Menna turns on the radio and begins to hum along. Cole smiles, lulled by the sound. After a moment, "So what were you thinking of?"

"Huh?" Menna turns to look at her. The girl is so young and fragile looking beside her. *Thirteen already,* she thinks to herself as she watches the wind from the open window tousle the girl's red hair.

"You said you were lost in thought," Cole points out. "What were you thinking?"

Menna turns and regards the girl in a sad sort of way. "About the past."

"What about the past?" her interest is instantly piqued. She loves stories of Menna's past. Menna cringes. She is not always so fond of recalling those moments.

"Just remembering some things I haven't thought about in a while," she says.

"Like what? Tell me about it," Cole says.

"Sweetie, you have heard every story fifteen times," Menna groans as she switches the radio station.

Cole falls silent for a moment, staring straight ahead, face blank. The silence in the car grows thicker and more disconcerting by the minute. Menna shifts in her seat, trying to wake her tiring legs. Cole stares straight ahead. Menna turns to the girl and smiles. Cole stares straight ahead. Menna tickles her right above her waist, but Cole bats her hand away.

"Sweetie we are both tired and grumpy, why don't we find a motel and get some sleep," she suggests.

"We stopping already?" Cole asks.

"Already?" Menna asks in mid-yawn. "It's four A.M. Honey, we've been driving for almost sixteen hours straight."

"Want me to take over?" Cole smiles.

"No, I want to get gas, some breakfast and then maybe stop to sleep for a while," Menna forces a weak smile, but she is too tired to be genuine.

Cole senses her mood, falls silent, as they patiently wait for the next gas station. When it finally approaches, they stop, and she yawns, then declares she has to go to the bathroom and slips quietly out the passenger door. Menna watches her go, smiling at the auburn hair that swishes as she walks. *So much of her mother in her.*

Menna pumps the gas, not really even watching the numbers until the valve shuts off, alerting her that the tank is full. She removes the nozzle and walks inside to pay. Walking in the door, she abruptly halts and stares at the man behind the counter.

He is young, twenty maybe, clean shaven with a snake tattoo strangling him. His hair is long and greasy, tied back with rogue strands covering his face. "Can I help yous?" he asks with a voice much gentler then she anticipates.

She hands him money and gawks for another moment. He makes change and meets her confused stare. "Something wrong?"

"Uh, uh, I was just wondering how much longer it'll be till I hit a diner or something, a motel maybe," she says.

"The next exit," he explains, "Roanoke. I reckon there is tons there."

His accent reminds her of how far she has driven, and she backs out of the station wordlessly.

Cole is in the car when she gets back in. "Menna?" she says, her tone asking, *What's wrong?*

"Yeah, sweetie?" she says, starting the engine without looking at the girl.

"You look like you saw a ghost in there," Cole says.

"No, honey, just someone who looked real familiar."

Cole giggles. "I can tell we're getting close to your home, I can hear your accent a little."

Menna shoots her an angry look before she realizes, then settles back in her seat. Cole begins to look out the window at the areas of land the sun has already reached. "What's the nearest city to where you grew up?"

"Mobile," Menna says as she begins to tap the wheel again. "But Mobile was a world away."

"Did you go to school there?"

"No, in town."

"Did you get good grades?"

"Not really."

"Then why do I have to?" Cole is staring at the window, glancing at Menna tentatively.

"Cole, you are smarter than I have ever been, and I refuse to see you not do something with it," Menna says. She braces herself for the normal argument that follows this, but Cole just sighs.

"You look sleepy."

Menna sighs. "I am."

Cole glances at her bracelet and smiles. "Why don't you tell me about him to keep yourself awake."

Menna grimaces. "You aren't going to let this go, are you?" she asks.

"If you really want me to."

She can tell Cole's feelings are hurt, so promises to tell her all the stories she can stand to hear after they have had some sleep.

They locate the motel and pull into the parking lot. They have to wake the sleepy desk clerk to check-in. He looks as though he is not only unaccustomed to customers this late at night, but unaccustomed to customers in general.

Cole carries bags upstairs, while Menna runs a bath. She needs to wash the dirt from the road off her body before she can sleep. The bathtub takes forever to fill up. Eventually she stops it halfway and climbs in.

Menna lays in the bathtub letting the water wash over her.

The water is hot, scalding almost, but feels good regardless.

Cole knocks on the door. "They just brought us more towels," she calls into the room, then slides the door open and throws a pile of white linen onto the floor.

Menna thanks her reflexively, then dunks under the water again. Closing her eyes helps her to block out the décor of the motel room, which seems too sterile, too white, too clean for this place.

Home sweet home, she thinks. She is suddenly so tired that her eyes begin to close despite her efforts. The water also recedes from her skin, but then rises and goes to the mirror.

Damn this place.

Max

When Menna and I were young, we were only faintly aware of how the rest of the town looked at us with a mixture of pity and disgust. We had never known anything outside of this town, and had never been treated in any way other than what we knew from its inhabitants. Thus, we never knew there was another way. We didn't see many of our classmates outside of school, and so we never saw the way they interacted with the adults. Menna's world was my world, and our fate was shared.

Nearly forty-five minutes outside of Mobile, we were far from an urban environment. The town, all in all, had five main streets, four traffic lights, and six police officers. There was no Main Street, oddly enough, but Maple Avenue was the primary stretch of road. It held a coffee shop, a grocery and deli, and a few scattered office buildings. Situated around a park, it ran for three blocks, which contained three of the four traffic lights, and often felt bustling, though there surely were not enough people to bustle.

We had our town gossips, for sure. Milly, Reverend Roulard's wife, could often be found sitting out in front of the deli with Josephine Willis, a spinster who looked after an aunt that had been dying for as long as I had been alive. They spent most of the days, hot and cold, perched on that bench clucking at the passersby. We didn't spend much time on Maple, but by age ten I had noticed that they both fell silent if Menna and I passed by. Milly looked at us with more pity, while Josephine did not attempt to conceal her disgust.

At the far end of Maple ran Thorton Street, which twisted down over the creek and out towards the woods. At the far end of Thorton was a tiny cul-de-sac, and at the far end of the cul-de-sac was a tiny two bedroom house that we lived in.

There were no other houses on the cul-de-sac. In fact, the nearest house was almost a mile up Thorton Street. We were isolated from this tiny town by distance, and kept apart from them by our mother.

The only memory I have of my mother, the only memory of her as I like to imagine she was supposed to be, is of the summer when I was ten. It was, by far, the longest stretch of her sobriety during my youth.

When she was sober, my mother was strikingly beautiful. It was from her that Lily inherited her flaming red hair and pale skin. My mother had a spray of perfect, light brown freckles across her nose and cheeks, and vivacious green eyes. Her accent was somehow lighter than everyone else's in our town, and when she was sober, her head was held a little higher. The only attribute of hers I emulated, by then, was her speech. Like her, I tried to say "not" instead of "ain't," because even drunk, she could sometimes sound smart.

Our last day of school that year, Menna and I had returned home to an empty house. Who knew where Lily was, but my mother was, presumably, at work. She had been gone each day we'd returned for weeks now, a sure sign that she liked this new job.

After being fired from the gas station down past Dark Street in May, she had gotten an office job two towns over. It was a half an hour drive each way, but a new place where she was simply Becca, and not the drunk, not the mother of that fiery Lily, or the grungy twins who wandered the streets clutching each other. Just Becca.

Now, as an adult, I know what that must have meant to her— being the office manager and not the drunk—but as a child, it only meant a safer home when she was at work, and a passing interest in us.

The first day of summer vacation dawned to the smell of cooking eggs and the distinctive hissing of coffee brewing. At the time, however, it wasn't distinctive to us.

"What is that?" Menna whispered. The attic seemed so full of heat that I thought surely the faded paint would melt from the walls, but that was typical of the summer. I had thought she was sleeping, and I looked over to find that her eyes were still shut.

"I think Momma is making coffee," I told her.

My stomach rumbled audibly. Missing breakfast, and usually lunch, was the norm during the summer. Lily unobtrusively ensured that there was dinner on the table each night, though she was rarely around. The hunger this day, however, was oddly intense and likely precipitated by the smell of my mother cooking.

"It smells good," Menna said, her eyes still squeezed shut as though she was terrified to open them and disrupt what must have been a dream.

"Let's go see what Momma is doing," I suggested. Menna finally opened her eyes, and we quickly headed down the stairs.

We entered the kitchen cautiously, and found her sitting there, coffee in hand, reading a newspaper. It was a scene most children in town were familiar with—Mom draped in a robe, the steam curling up from some weak, sugary coffee, across from two plates heaped with eggs and pancakes—but to us, this was unknown, and therefore dangerous.

"You two are up early," she said, a slight lilt to her voice, her words crisp and clear. She didn't look up from the paper, but nodded towards the plates across from her.

We quietly moved across the kitchen floor to the table, and climbed into the chairs across from her. Neither of us spoke, and we ate quietly, but quickly, as though this was a dream that might suddenly vanish.

"What will you be doing in school today?" she asked finally, folding the paper and setting it on the floor beside her.

We looked at each other for a moment before Menna answered. "It's the first day of summer break, Momma," she said.

"Is it June already?" she asked, staring whimsically out the window.

"Almost July," I said meekly. The school had flooded that winter, which had been unusually cold. We had a two-week break in the middle of February, which they had tacked on to the end of the year. The weeks had been misery, with Nick in school, and it being too cold to be outside.

"Oh," my mother replied. She stood and gathered her robe around her. It was tattered terrycloth, much too warm for the season. It was not yet eight and the air in the house was teeming with moisture and heat. "When will I get your grades?" she asked.

Menna and I both stared at her blankly. She had never looked at our grades before. I wasn't entirely sure she could have told you what grade we were in. Most of the time Menna and I only made it to school because the counselor had gotten in the habit of coming to pick us up in the morning.

"Hello?" she said finally, a hint of anger entering her voice. "I asked you a question."

Menna stared at her plate as she answered. "They usually take about a week or two, but Max probably got straight As, and I think I got a few Bs and Cs."

Momma seemed to think about this for a moment, once again staring out the window. "Max, I don't know where that brain of yours comes from, but it sure ain't from me." She said this sadly, and then turned to look at me. My ears burned red and I was furious with Menna for what she had said. I also had this sudden desire to ask her, beg her, to tell me if my brain came from my father, and who he might be, and how I could find him. She was sober, she was calm. Maybe she would tell us, maybe she knew where he was. But I swallowed the urge, and instead sullenly said, "I don't know, Momma," I muttered. "I just try hard is all."

"And you, Menna, you don't try hard?" she asked, and I felt both a wave of panicked protectiveness for my sister and relief that the attention had been diverted from me.

"I do, Momma," Menna said, staring her full in the face. I was amazed by her fearlessness. "I'm just not as smart as Max."

Momma seemed to accept that, and moved towards the door of the kitchen. "I'll be working late tonight," she informed us, "so I left some money in the drawer. Go up to the store and get yourself some sandwiches or something."

The silence that pervaded after she left was stranger than her presence. Menna and I quickly and wordlessly ran for the door lest she emerge from her bedroom suddenly drunk and angry.

We ran to the field and into the woods, but stopped a short way on the other side of the tree line. "What was that all about?" Menna demanded, as though I might have some secret insight she lacked.

"She hasn't been drinking much, lately," I offered.

"I sure hope she starts again soon," Menna said, half to herself.

"What the heck would you say that for?" I asked, punching her lightly in the arm.

"She's doesn't ask us so many questions when she's drunk. Mostly, she leaves us alone," Menna explained. I was surprised that she didn't hit me back—that would have been typical—instead she rubbed her arm, though I suspect it was actually her pride that ached.

"Mostly, but at least she doesn't hit us when she's sober," I pointed out. I grimaced, thinking back to a few days in the fall where I had an eye so swollen and bruised that looking at the blackboard in class had made me dizzy. I can't remember why she had hit me. Truth be told, I can't remember her hitting me that often, nor Menna. But the rage that Lily endured reverberated through the house and made it hard to breath sometimes.

Menna nodded and looked around. "I hate the hot," she said, wiping sweat from her forehead with the back of her hand. "When I am eighteen, I am moving away to New York." Her declaration was emphatic, and she began to walk away.

"Why New York?" I asked her.

"My teacher said it snows there, and there is stuff to do all night long," she explained, walking farther ahead of me.

When I remember this day, I remember the dirt on my sister's shirt, and how her hair hung around her in greasy clumps. I remember that mine was too long, and equally filthy. I remember that my shoes didn't quite fit—they never did when I was younger—and that my pants were a size too big and kept slipping down. Much like dinner often appeared, so did new clothes with blue plastic rings that signified they found their way to us from the Salvation Army. Lily, likewise, never acknowledged that she did these things, and perhaps she didn't. Perhaps this too, was an act of the rarely seen Becca who was so often overshadowed by the drunk.

That day, however, I saw no stains and felt no shame over the grease in my hair. I was full, which was an unusual feeling for this early in the morning, and rested. My sister plowed on ahead of me, always approaching the hill as though she had some silent order she had to follow.

We headed further into the forest, emerging at last at the hill. Nick sat where he always did—halfway up, leaning back on his elbows, eyes closed. I sometimes wondered if he was a statue there who awakened when we arrived. This was the start of our third summer coming here, and we had never found him absent.

We trudged up to meet him, taking a seat on either side of him, and waiting for him to speak. He didn't open his eyes before he said, "You two were in school forever. Did they hold you back?"

"No!" I said angrily, hearing a touch of Menna's pride in my own voice.

Menna sighed and rolled her eyes and launched into the tale of the flood. Once she was done, she fell backwards dramatically and stared at the sky.

The clouds were moving quickly that day, and though it was early, the sky seemed to be darkening in preparation for dusk. "It's going to rain," Nick prophesied, though he hadn't yet opened his eyes.

"How do you know?" Menna demanded.

"The stones told me," he said, thus beginning the summer as we had finished the last—gently teasing. Menna elbowed him in the ribs but didn't say anything.

"What do we do if it rains?" I asked.

"We get wet," he said simply, and that was the only answer we required.

We fell into our normal routine, which was simple, but ours. Most kids our age probably played with toys or watched TV or found a playground. We had none of those things, nor had we ever, so we talked, and daydreamed.

"Nick, did you come here every day before you met us?" Menna asked as the afternoon sun began to climb high above us and pour thick, wet heat over us.

"There are lots of places I go during the day," he said. His answers so often answered nothing, but we rarely pressed on, sensing some wisdom behind his words that was far beyond his age.

"Ain't you got friends over there?" I asked, nodding towards the other side of the hill where the fence stood.

"I have friends," he said, "but they are mostly older. There aren't many of us over there, not anymore." There was a sad silence then. Finally, he added, "And my friends have mostly moved away, like everyone does."

"You moving away?" Menna asked. There was a sudden muted panic in her voice. She expressed what I felt, then, a bewildered fear of what would fill our days if Nick wasn't here anymore.

He smiled a bit and turned to face us both. "I am too young to go anywhere. I'm stuck . . . with you two." Nick playfully reached over and pushed me on the shoulder. Menna fumed, I could see, but I felt happy and acknowledged by our one and only friend.

Menna

All that summer, we waited and waited for my mother to start drinking again. We tiptoed around, tried to always answer her with "please" and "thank you" and be on our best behavior when she was around, as though somehow our actions could prevent what was inevitable, or perhaps delay it a bit at least.

Max told me, that first night after we had woken to find her cooking and drinking coffee, that maybe it would last long enough for her to reveal to us who our father was. The idea filled me with fear. I wanted to know, so desperately. I had dreams of a tall, blond man with blue eyes pulling up in a shiny new car and whisking us away to some place where no one drank and you never had to go to school in dirty, too-small clothes. I imagine it was the dream most orphans had, and I truly felt like an orphan, one parent stolen by ignorance, and the other drowning in a bottle.

And yet, what if simply by asking, by making her think about something that she clearly despised, what if that was enough to get her drinking again. It seemed safer not to mention it, but I understood his desire, the pull to ask her. Sometimes I wondered if I felt the way Max felt because we were so similar, if I was able to feel for him. He kept so silent and sullen, and I thought, then, that maybe he needed me to help him feel.

37

And the sobriety held much longer than we could have antici-
pated. Through June and July she had appeared each morning,
cooked breakfast, drank her coffee, and dressed for work. Initially
she followed the pattern of questions, which we could only answer
tersely for there was little to tell.

"What will you guys do today?" she would ask, not looking up
from her paper.

"Nothing," we would always say, and it was mostly true. We
would do nothing, but something told us not to tell her about Nick.
Max perhaps felt that way out of fear for how she would react. I
somehow felt that Nick and our hill were apart from this house,
from my sometimes-sober mother, and I didn't want to bring her
into it.

"You two don't cause trouble, do you?" She still didn't look up,
asking the warning question as casually as though she were reading
us the weather report.

"No, Momma," I would say. Max stared down. Maybe he
thought hanging out with an Indian was her definition of getting
into trouble.

As she walked out every morning to dress for work, she would
toss directions for a dinner or a promise to be home to cook over
her shoulder. She had been true to these promises for the past six
weeks. We simply wondered when she would finally fall short.
Already, then, at age ten we knew that this was a question of *when*
and not *if.* The house was eerily calm, and I often felt uneasy to
notice that the smell of cheap whiskey was obviously absent.

Lily was also frequently absent from our lives. Her fights with
my mother often grew violent when my mother was drunk, but
they were short and quickly forgotten. When my mother was sober,
however, the fights were more arguments, and, though largely
based on unspoken animosity, they cast a tense web over the
house.

Not having Lily around, sulking and brooding aside, was as
odd as my mother's sobriety.

That was a particularly violent hurricane year. Typically, the
storms were nothing but overheard conversations in the stores

around town to us, but that summer there seemed to be a tropical storm threatening every other week.

Early in August, we padded down the stairs to the kitchen to find my mother sitting there again. We were on the verge of calling this a habit, of becoming accustomed to seeing her waiting for us. Two plates of eggs sat across from her, and we dove in to eat.

"There's going to be a bad storm today," she said, "so you two stick near this house."

"We're always near," I said, and Max stared down at his plate. This was another half-truth.

"Max," my mother said. She looked up from her paper and stared across at him sternly. "You know you have to take care of your sister always, right?"

My temper immediately flared, and I took her words as an insinuation that I couldn't take care of myself. Then I noticed the intensity of her stare on Max, and Max met her stare with an equal intensity. Before I could open my mouth to protest, Max nodded once and Momma went back to her paper. As her face disappeared behind the front page, she simply said, "It's a good thing, you know, you two having each other."

I turned to look at Max, but his face was on his plate again. We didn't speak until we jointly greeted Nick when we arrived at the hill an hour later.

"You guys are late," he said tonelessly. "I've been waiting."

"Well, Momma cooked breakfast again," I said, flopping on to the grass beside him. I noticed Max still standing there, a few feet down the hill. He kept looking to Nick, and then to me, and then looking away. This pattern continued all morning, as though Max wanted to speak with Nick but wouldn't do it with me there. I wondered frequently until the early afternoon if this had something to do with what had transpired with my mother in the kitchen this morning.

"Eggs again today?" Nick asked with a hint of teasing in his voice. It seemed to be the only thing my mother could cook. In actuality, it is the only dish I'd ever seen her cook. Even that summer, cooking dinner involved something frozen and heated.

"What else?" I asked. Max tired of staring at us and sat down by Nick's feet, looking into the trees.

"My mom used to cook breakfast for us," Nick said. "She always made sweet potato pancakes and bacon on Sundays." He sounded whimsical and sad, as though he was speaking more to himself than to us.

"She doesn't cook no more?" I asked.

"No," he said simply. He laid back and closed his eyes.

We sat in silence for a long time, made lazy by the heat and the sun, and a lack of anything in our little lives to say to each other. Then, the sky suddenly turned black and a refreshing but unsettling chill seemed to flood the clearing.

"You two need to get home," he said, suddenly standing and scanning the trees.

"Why?" I asked, jumping up beside him.

"It's going to rain," he said, and began walking up the hill away from us.

"We've been out here in the rain before," I yelled after him.

Nick turned to face me, smiling. Though still in his early teens, he sometimes looked like such a man. "Not rain like this," he said, and he trotted off away from us.

By the time Max and I reached our house, it seemed to be fully night outside, and the wind whipped my hair around wildly. As we opened the front gate, which hung to the ground limply, fat rain drops spattered against us and we heard a distant crack of thunder.

Max ran immediately onto the porch and didn't realize that I stayed behind until he opened the front door and I didn't come in after him. I stood very still in the middle of the front lawn, feeling the rain pound down on me. It was the first time all summer I hadn't felt the heat folding around me like a blanket, and I relished it.

"Menna, what are you doing?" Max screamed from the porch. His voice strained and I barely heard him over the howling wind, but I could see from his face that he was concerned. We were less than twelve feet apart, but the space between us seemed immense and unusual.

"It feels nice!" I screamed back and beckoned to him to come to me.

Max ventured out onto the lawn, the awning from the porch still shielding him slightly from the rain. "This isn't safe, Menna," he said. His face had grown as dark as the sky.

"I like the rain," I said. The water was cool yet violent. I stared at my ragged shoes, seeing dirt from my skin slide down my knees to pool at my feet.

Another peel of thunder, much closer, echoed around us. I glanced up once more at the cloud-filled sky and darted up on the porch.

"You are crazy as a bed bug," Max said, and we entered the house.

As we shook off in the small foyer area, I looked up to notice that Lily was sitting quietly on the couch. An empty glass bottle sat on the table before her. I stepped closer to see the tears running down her cheeks.

"Lily, you all right?" I asked.

Her eyes moved towards me, though her head stayed perfectly still. "She drank this whole thing last night," she said, leaning her head towards the bottle. "So much for a peaceful summer."

I was surprised to hear her say it, as the summer had seemed to be anything but peaceful for her and my mother. They bickered, and argued, and often resorted to the silent treatment for days on end. But, Lily must have felt as Max did—it was better than being hit. And, while Lily did yell and back talk more than Max and I would have dreamed of, she also got hit way more often than we did as well.

"Maybe it was just that one bottle," Max offered, but he couldn't hide the disbelief in his own voice.

Lily stared directly at him, as though he was some stranger she was meeting for the first time. "How old are you now, Max?" she asked, though she well knew. Two cupcakes had magically appeared on our birthday, each with the number ten boldly printed on them.

"I'm ten," Max said.

Lily shook her head. "I've only got two more years of this. I feel sorry for you two."

"What do you mean, two more years?" I asked, stepping forward into the room.

"I am eighteen in two years, and I am out of here," she promised. "I would leave now if I could, and not deal with you fucking ragamuffins anymore." As she got up and walked out the front door, she knocked into me, nearly knocking me to the floor.

I settled back against the wall. The door caught behind her, letting in a gust of wind and a deluge of water. I wondered where she was going. I wondered what on earth was keeping her from leaving now, as it certainly wasn't my mother.

I pulled the door closed behind her.

"Why is she so mean?" Max asked. We never discussed the mysterious food that found its way into the house, or the new clothes that periodically were folded on the floor of our room at night. Maybe it was my mother. Maybe Lily really did hate us so much.

"She's gonna get lost in this storm," I said, and another crack of thunder preceded the house going dark.

"No power," Max whispered.

"You think Momma can drive in this?" I asked.

"No," he said simply. We had no flashlights, no candles. We had eaten breakfast that morning, and so neither of us was particularly hungry. We headed to the attic silently.

It was nearly three o'clock in the afternoon, hours before Momma normally arrived home. We both curled up on the floor and silently listened to the rain hit the roof. Moments before, as I had stood outside, the storm had felt like it was here to wash me, wash us, clean the house. Max had stood there, with my mother's direction to protect me, wanting to pull me back into it, to the dirt.

Now, with the knowledge of that glass bottle down the stairs and on the table, the absence of my mother and my sister, the silence of my brother, the storm seemed to be lashing me to the floor inside this house, inside all of it. I was tied here, in this dank and dirty room, with no one but my brother.

My momma didn't come home that night, nor did Lily. Max and I waited out the storm together in the attic, watching the rain beat on the windows. The roof began to leak through the night, and we had to find new spots to sleep where we wouldn't get wet.

In the morning, we wandered to the hill together, our stomachs empty for the first time in weeks. The air smelled fresh and new, and the grass was still wet and a vibrant green. Nick was there waiting, as he always was, though he seemed uncharacteristically anxious to see us.

"How'd you guys fare through the storm?" he asked as soon as we were within ear shot.

Max looked at me and stood by silently. I opened my mouth to tell Nick about it, but somehow anything I could tell him seemed too big to fit through my mouth.

The next time I saw my mother she was drunk.

Chapter Three

*M*ax isn't even out of the driveway before he is hit by an intense pang of loneliness. He can't remember the last time he was even this far away from her, out from under the warmth and contentment that she laid across him. He considers turning around already, going back, slamming the door that had been so quickly opened last night by a simple phone call.

Max, my brother, I need you.

Was that still him, he wonders, her brother. Was that boy, seventeen and already weary, still within him somewhere?

The sun is still far away from the desert, but its orange hues have begun to touch the sand around him. He drives fast, hoping more distance, more time, more miles of sand between them will cure him of this guilt for leaving, the guilt for needing to, the guilt for never having once, before this day, worried like he was now of what had happened to his sister.

And now he is leaving again. The woman who had kept him together for the past three years. Netis, who had clung to him last night, made love to him last night, driven by the intense fear of his departure, and confusion as to its reason.

The first thing that had struck him about Netis was how much she looked like Nick, he muses as more miles pass by him, in the obvious and very unobvious ways. Surely, they shared the same long, thick, black hair, black eyes, wide mouth. They were both oddly tall in comparison to everyone around them, and both moved lithely and soberly through a crowd.

But it was something more than that, something he had noticed the very second she served him that first drink when he wondered into the small bar on the side of the highway.

"Passing through?" she asked. The glass was sweating and already nearly warm by the time it made it across the room to him. She, too, was sweating, her dark hair pulled back into a high-pony-tail.

The heat, her hair, the smoothness of her voice, had made him feel nostalgic and simultaneously tired.

"Something like that," he had responded and downed his drink in one swallow.

Her voice had instantly changed into a hard, disdainful lilt. "Sure as hell look like you belong." He had looked around then, at the other patrons. A mix of Indians and whites, all alone, all staring at empty glasses with empty eyes.

"Seems like you've got me pegged already," he had spat back angrily, indignant by the comparison and yet somehow intrigued by her.

Her face softened a bit then, though never quite reached apolo-getic. "Where you headed to?" she asked. She sat down across from him then in one, quick motion. The other men bristled as she did, as if out of fear of the delay this would cause in their refills.

"California," he said.

"Where in California?"

He stared at her hard for a moment. She sat with entitlement, as though she had every right to demand the information. "Don't know yet," he said finally.

"Just figuring it out as you go, then?" she asked, the bite returning to her voice.

He had known her less than three minutes then, and already the bickering seemed normal to him, natural and comfortable. She acted as though she had the right to know his plans, and he felt compelled to share them. It unnerved him and soothed him all at once and he smiled despite himself.

"I'm a writer. I can do what I do just about anywhere, and I needed a change of venue," he said.

She had seemed to accept that, nodding quietly, before she got up and wandered back to the bar to pour more rye for her patrons, seldom taking her eyes off of Max.

He had stayed until closing, only drinking one more drink, but watching her as she watched him. There was a calmness in her movements, an easiness in the way she interacted with everyone around her. As the bar closed, and she finished cleaning, she walked back over to him. "I'm Netis," she said.

"Max," he said. He stood, then, realizing that he had to leave, though something in him didn't want to.

"Hope to see you again, Max," she had said, a half-smile spreading across her face.

That was the last night he had spent without her until now, and he worried, as he drove, that another man might enter the bar tonight. Someone less sullen, less secretive, and that he would find the same comfortable banter with her. Someone else might be there when he came back.

And I will go back, he promised himself, looking forward over a long stretch of desert, and wondering what he would find waiting for him in Alabama.

Max

Three weeks before the eighth grade ended, my principal sponsored an award assembly for the school. This happened every year and I had never been. I imagined one of those polite affairs with stale cookies and unsweetened Kool-aid, standing with my teachers, desperate to think of something to say, anything to talk about.

Two days before the assembly my teacher, Mrs. Walsh, called me to the front of the room during a test. I had finished some time before and handed her my paper, relishing the chance to sit at my desk and read.

"Max, come out into the hallway with me," she said. I glanced back over my shoulder at Menna, who was still struggling with arithmetic. She shot me an annoyed look, I knew it ate her up that I always finished first. My moment of gloating immediately gave way to confusion about what conversation was waiting in the hallway. That was the last year we were in classes together. After that we were bused to a larger high school, nearly half an hour away, and our only time together was the bus ride.

On that day, my sister's annoyance made me feel also guilty. I hated watching her struggle with something that was so easy to me. As much as I loved being better at her at something, it also made me uncomfortable that school was the only part of our lives that we couldn't share. I was almost grateful to Mrs. Walsh for getting me out of the room and away from this awkward feeling. Nonetheless, my face immediately began to burn as I tried to imagine what I had done wrong.

Throughout the entire year I had spoken maybe ten words to Mrs. Walsh outside of answering her questions when she called on me. I wondered if she had graded my test already and would accuse me of cheating. I wasn't sure how to tell her that her tests were some of the easiest I had ever taken.

When we reached the hallway, she closed the door with a gentle push of her hand. It thudded, a soft sound that echoed like thunder through the abandoned hallway.

"Are you coming to the principal's ceremony on Thursday?" she asked.

"No," I said.

"I would like you to," she said. "I read the stories you wrote for Ms. Jenson's class. You are very talented, Max."

Ms. Jenson was the English teacher. She had recognized three weeks into the year that I had read all of the books on our reading list, and most from the ninth grade's list as well, and had given me a series of creative projects to occupy me while the rest of the class plodded through *Romeo and Juliet*. The projects had resulted in two finished short pieces, one a fantasy about an enchanted sword and one a simple story about an Indian boy searching for his family in the old West.

"Thank you," I said, still wary of this woman's true intentions and angry at Ms. Jenson for sharing my work. Other than the teacher, only Menna had ever read anything I wrote. Menna poured over each page as I finished scribbling the words on them and smiled at me at the parts she liked.

"I want you to read one of your stories at the assembly," she said.

"OK," I blurted out before thinking about it. It was not in my nature to say no to a teacher, but this request terrified me. "But can I pick which story I want to read?"

"Absolutely," she said. "Be here at six, Max, and wear something nice, a suit if you have one."

I didn't have a suit. I didn't have anything nice to wear, period.

Menna glanced up at me inquisitively as I walked back to the room and sat at my desk, but I didn't meet her gaze. It wasn't until later than night that I relayed the encounter to Menna as we sprawled out on the attic floor, preparing for sleep.

"So you're going to read your story?" she asked.

"I guess," I said.

"I told you so," she said.

"Told me what?"

"That you're smart," she said. Normally she taunted me with this accusation, but on that night she just smiled softly before she closed her eyes to go to sleep.

"What should I read?" I asked.

"The one with the Indian boy," she said, her eyes still closed.

Menna awoke early the next day and told Lily that I would be speaking in front of the whole school. Our older sister rolled her eyes in her usual fashion, but that night she appeared at home with a white, button down shirt.

"Everyone knows you're my brother," she explained, "so I won't have you standing up in front of the whole school looking grungy."

The shirt had a yellow stain over the right breast pocket and was easily three sizes too big for me but, when tucked into my best jeans (or the only pair that wasn't torn) it made me feel respectable.

Menna walked me to school that night.

"You coming to hear me?" I asked her.

"Yeah, I need to go do something," she said. "I'll be back." She kissed me on the cheek quickly and darted away. I felt naked without her at my side as I walked in.

For an hour I stood back stage of the auditorium and looked at the other kids who were involved. I was the only one reading a story, but some kids were singing, or presenting awards.

Kay, a black girl from my class, was there. She looked very adult in a black skirt and white shirt, definitely cleaner and more assembled than I was.

"You reading, Max?" she asked.

"Yeah."

She smiled. "I write stories, too," she said before disappearing into a group of her friends.

I took the stage at 7:30 and squinted at the lights, trying desperately to locate my sister. Finally I found her and saw that, in her lap, she held something proudly, eagerly.

I smiled and began to read.

My story was six pages long. I was on page four when the audience began to shift in their seats. The noise made me nervous. I stuttered a bit, stumbled over a word.

On page five, there was a cough, a sigh, which made me long to find myself on the last sentence. I took a brief pause, and looked up to find Menna's face in the crowd. She looked at me hopefully and encouragingly. I went on, my voice strong again.

By page the top of page six there were muted whispers of impatience rolling throughout the auditorium. I began to panic. When I reached the last sentence, I heard it. A loud, grating voice from the black space saying, "Shut the hell up, kid." Someone shushed the voice violently and I rushed through the last few words and ducked off stage before the haphazard applause began.

The wings were, thankfully, as dark as the space beyond the stage. I sat quickly as the next kid moved to the podium, and buried my head in my hands, wondering why I had agreed to do this.

"Max." A voice drew me out of my self-pity. I looked up to find Kay staring at me. "I liked your story," she whispered before stepping onto the stage.

I stood and walked farther into the wings. Our principal was standing there waiting for me. "Hello Max," he said in a deep, stiff voice. I wondered instantly if I was in trouble for taking too long or rushing the end.

"Hello," I said.

"Thank you for agreeing to read your story," he said.

"You're welcome."

"You're very talented, Max," he said.

"Thank you," I said.

"Do you write your stories out long-hand?"

"Yes, sir, I do."

He smiled. "I have an old typewriter in my office. It isn't one of the new electronic ones or anything, but if you promise to keep writing this summer, you may have it."

"Wow, thank you sir," I said.

He smiled and headed towards the stage. I walked out into the hallway; Menna was waiting for me there. The item from her lap turned to be a ragged pile of flowers, which she presented to me shyly.

"Stupid Jimmy Reid," Menna said, hugging me and mashing her gift between us.

"Was that him, telling me to shut up?"

"Yeah, it was, and I could just punch him," Menna's face began to grow red with anger. I put my arm around her, silently telling her it was OK.

"He's the mayor's son, Menna, so there is no use getting mad. He does what he wants, says what he wants."

She nodded silently and we turned and walked out. The applause for the next students thundered behind us as we walked out of the back doors.

I picked up my typewriter the next day. Menna came with me to the principal's office, but waited outside the door, looking nervous and fidgety. The principal walked me out, the beast of a typewriter balanced precariously in my arms. He nodded at Menna, and I looked at her in profile. My sister was beautiful. Our faces were nearly the same, though her long hair slid around her shoulders. She was tall and thin, somewhat gangly but with a determined set to her shoulder and eyes.

Menna nodded back to the principal, and walked ahead to open the door for me. I struggled through the door, and the whole way home.

That summer I began to keep a journal. It began in the moments after we returned from the hill and Nick, typing on old paper I found in a box behind the library. Daily, I would create notes about our conversations, about what I thought, felt, how the summer went.

I began to write more and more stories from there. As I began to type, I found that I had more stories than I could get onto the paper in an hour or two an evening. I began to write in the mornings as well, with a crazed hurry to get out as many pages as I could before Menna was ready to go to the hill.

It was only a matter of weeks after school let out before I became too engrossed in what I was writing to go with Menna. For the first time our lives, we spent hours apart.

Menna

It was very hot the day Max decided not to come outside with me. "I want to finish this story," he explained, barely looking up from his typewriter.

I had grown to hate that thing in the weeks since he had lugged it home. Before that, Max frequently had his nose stuck in a book, but he almost always only read in the mornings before I woke up. Now, with the typewriter, it was mornings and evenings, every spare moment with his fingers working away.

Two days before we had come home early from the hill so he could start on a story. The day before we didn't leave the house until nearly eleven because his idea had blossomed. He fed sheet after sheet of scrap paper into it and banged away.

When I woke up that morning I resolved to convince him to leave right away, but he was already up, scribbling on the sheets he had written.

"I was waiting for you to wake up," he said when he noticed my eyes were open.

"Great," I said, "let's go."

"I was waiting so I didn't wake you up with my typing," he said, once again not looking at me and feeding a sheet into his machine. I stared for a long time, waiting for him to look up and see me, to see the hurt and frustration in my face. He didn't, and so I wandered downstairs alone.

The living room was littered with empty cans and bottles. Lily was asleep on the couch, her red hair splayed out across the pillow. She was wearing shorts and the white tank top she had been wearing the day before when we got home. She looked peaceful and quiet, her face resting on her hand. I looked back at her for a moment before ducking outside, thinking to myself how pretty she really was. As I closed the door, I heard Max begin striking the keys on his typewriter, heard Lily stir and curse under her breath. I was at the gate before the fight began.

I sat on the porch for almost an hour, not quite sure what to do with myself. I felt oddly incomplete without Max. He was so often silent and aloof, oddly hovering but rarely saying much, and yet, he was always *there*.

Ultimately, though, my wondering was short-lived and I felt an odd pull towards the hill, where I knew Nick would be waiting. I was nervous, however, as I moved through the trees, that he would ask where Max was and be annoyed that I had come alone. In the summers that had been spent here, swinging, talking, trading items, laughing, playing, it had always been the three of us. Max's absence clung to me.

Nick was one of the last few items that truly belonged to *us*. The days, our room, our classes, even clothes used to be items shared freely and out of necessity. Max had taken to sleeping on the couch any night where our mother actually fell asleep in her bed, and the damned typewriter was certainly his. At twelve, I was old enough now to need my own clothes, mostly Lily's hand-me-downs, and we had been placed in different classes next year.

It felt like something of a betrayal now, going to see Nick without my brother, but my world during the summers revolved around this hill and I couldn't let my day go by wasted.

Nick sat quietly on a swing at the top of the hill when I arrived. That was unusual. He was almost always sitting halfway up, half leaning, half lying. He looked odd to me on the swing, but this was a day of oddities. I paused at the foot of the hill, feeling a momentary nervousness before starting up. Would he leave when I arrived without Max? What would we talk about? Typically, Nick and I did most of the talking anyway, but Max was there and his presence facilitated our talking.

"Has Max officially married his typewriter?" he asked as I slunk up the hill. Nick was fifteen now, with thick arms and the threat of a beard on his face. His hair was pulled back and he had truly begun to look like the man he had always behaved like. Even then I wondered why he spent so much time with us, though I suppose there were no more appealing options.

"Yeah, the idiot," I said, flopping onto the swing beside him. "Guess everyone has better things to do this summer than hang out with me." Lily was about to turn 18, and spoke often of her dreams of moving out the second the clock struck midnight.

Nick smiled and said, "I don't."

"What do you do when you aren't here?" I asked him.

"I go home, or hang out in the woods," he explained, nodding towards the trees that surrounded us. "What do you do?"

"I dunno. Max and I go home and to our room and talk. Or don't talk," I said. When we weren't here, Max and I just *were*.

"You feel weird without him here?" he asked.

"I guess. He's always with me, so when he isn't, I feel like I forgot something," I said.

"I always wondered that about you two, if you still existed without each other," he said.

"Yeah, I guess it's disappointing to just have me here," I said, suddenly blushing and realizing that my fear had been right. Nick wasn't interested in just seeing me. It bothered me inexplicably.

"No it isn't," he said. "You just look odd alone."

"Odd?" I rolled the word over in my mouth.

Before I began to wonder what he meant by odd, he continued. "I don't mean ugly or bad, Menna. I just mean different."

I had looked at him shyly then. I suddenly had the urge to ask if he didn't mean ugly, what he thought I was. It was a strange impulse, and one I quickly stifled. Nick glanced at me sideways and smiled softly to himself.

"What should we do today?" I asked him.

He looked startled. "What else would we do?" he asked. "Let's talk."

"OK," I said. We began to swing in silence. Maybe half an hour later I reached up after a while to ease some stray, sweat drenched strands of hair into my ponytail. "I can't wait to live somewhere that isn't so hot," I complained.

"And where is that?" he asked. "Where are you going to go when you can?"

"New York," I said quickly.

"You ever been before?"

"I've never been out of the state."

"So how do you know it has to be New York?"

I thought on that for a while. "I don't, I guess. It just seems like a good place to try. And there are lots of schools there, so Max can go to college and I can work."

"You aren't going to college?" he asked.

"Are you?" I spat back. I felt any questioning about school or my intentions from anyone was an accusation. I hated that I wasn't smart like Max, but hated school even more.

"No," he said, simply. "I don't much like school. I want to do something else."

"Me, too," I said.

"And what are you going to do?" he asked.

"I don't know," I admitted, honestly.

"You know, New York isn't the only place cooler than here," he said.

"Like where?" I asked.

"Maine?" he offered.

"I think Maine is *really* cold," I said.

He looked around. "Cold would be nice."

"Yeah," I admitted.

"And there is more space in Maine," he said.

"I like the idea of a city," I said.

"There are cities in Maine," he said.

"I could think about Maine," I said. "I do have some time before I have to make a decision, you know."

"I have a little bit. Molly is leaving soon, so she can let me know how New York is," he said.

"She going to school?" I asked.

"Yeah," he said sadly.

I smiled at him, and he smiled back.

Chapter Four

*M*enna is jolted awake by a knock at the door. Water splashes around her, and she realizes she has fallen asleep in the tub.

"Great, Menn, why not drown yourself on the way down," she says to herself as she rises from the water, wrinkled and red but somehow not feeling clean, and fumbles on the floor for a towel. She wraps herself up in it and walks out into the room.

Cole is sitting on the bed, fully dressed with the morning sun covering her, hitting buttons on a remote as she stares at, but does not watch, a small television on a shabby, falling apart dresser.

"You were in there for an hour. How dirty could you have been?" Cole asks, not looking up, but with interest in her voice.

"Not dirty, just tired," Menna says. She begins to look through her luggage for something to wear, but gives up almost instantly and crawls under the covers of the other bed in her towel.

"So you aren't going to finish the story yet, are you?" Cole asks, and now she looks up hopefully.

"When we get back on the road, I will tell you more," Menna promises, closing her eyes and hoping sleep overtakes her quickly.

A silence fills the musty room. The beds creak as they both turn and try to sleep. Finally, Cole's quiet voice whispers, "This is really hard for you, isn't it?"

Menna sighs. "It is," she says with finality.

"I'm sorry, Menna, I'm sorry I am making you do this."

She opens her eyes and finds this red-headed girl staring at her with grief and fear. Menna feels instantly guilty, the weight of what Cole didn't know falling heavily upon her. *Have I tried too hard to keep her happy?* she wonders. *Does she have the right to know more?*

Menna blinks hard, rubs her forehead with her palms, and sighs. *No,* she thinks. "Cole, you have a right to know about where you came from. I am just sorry I can't tell it all to you," Menna says. The girl seems to accept this and closes her eyes to sleep again.

After a moment, the silence is again broken. "Menna?"

"Yeah, honey," Menna says without opening her eyes.

"Why now?"

"Oh," Menna says as though she's just burned her hand.

"Well, I mean, I've asked before, and you've never wanted to talk. And you've never let me miss school before, not even when I was really sick," Cole begins to gush.

"I let you stay home when you're sick," Menna says. "And now just seemed like the time."

"Why do you need Max?"

"What do you mean?"

"You always handle everything. It was weird to hear you tell him on the phone that you need him," Cole says.

"During that conversation I was having when you were supposed to be sleeping?"

"Yes," is the quiet reply.

"It will all make sense, Cole, I promise," Menna says, and Cole senses the finality in her voice and goes to sleep.

Menna sets her alarm. *I will get up in four hours,* she thinks. *Maybe we can make it there by tonight.*

Max

Birthdays in my house were nonexistent. Menna and I knew ours was July 8, Lily's August 15, but neither date mattered. Just signified turning older, nothing else.

Until we turned fourteen.

Every summer morning, after showering and changing clothes, we would get up and head downstairs. Learning from the hurt face that Menna had shown me every time I didn't go to the hill the past summer, I had made an effort to be with her.

My mother had a new job that summer, and a new boyfriend, and seemed generally happy with her life. And as little as she had to do with us, when she was happy, it meant things were easier. We could sleep without listening to her fight with Lily, could walk around normally without fear that she would lash out, and there was almost always food in the house. She was drunk frequently, but in a quiet, contented way.

The week before she had even brought home cookies for us, and an old, battered TV she had seen in the Goodwill. It barely worked, but for once there was peace enough to sit in the living room and watch the fuzz.

"For my babies," she had said as she plunked it down across from our tattered, paisley couch that the stuffing fell out of when you sat on it. For a moment I had wondered who she was talking about when she said that. I had never heard her call us anything but mistakes.

That morning before work she stuck her head into the attic to wish us both happy birthdays. We didn't talk about that; I guess we figured we had been dreaming.

After breakfast we would head to the hill, where Nick would always be waiting. He always beat us there, no matter how early we got there, and usually left later then we did. Sometimes I wondered if he spent the night there.

Menna got up before I did that morning, and was fixing pancakes. She was suddenly in love with the idea of cooking and sewing, anything domestic. "One day I'm going to have a family to cook for, I better start learning how," she would say if I asked her about it.

She had a lot of learning to do. Her pancakes looked more like charcoal, but you couldn't tell her that. To her they were perfect.

She set the table with dishes and everything, even put out knives, which we didn't need as the pancakes crumbled as soon as you put your fork into them. She went outside to the yard and picked some wildflowers, though I couldn't imagine why. "What's with all this extravagant stuff?" I asked as I sat down.

"Huh?" Menna turned to look at me wearing her normal annoyed face, as she did whenever I used one of my dictionary words on her.

"The frilly junk, what's up with it?"

"I just thought it might be nice for our birthday," she said, though the mischievous smile on her face told me that she was lying.

"Do you want to invite Kay to come with us today?" she asked suddenly.

"Kay?" I asked. "Why would I invite Kay to come with us?"

Kay was my friend from school, and even there we didn't get to talk much. Sometimes I would run into her at the library, though, and that was always nice.

"Well, I asked Nick to bring Molly to the hill, it could be like a little party," she said.

"Molly?" I was a bit surprised that she mentioned Nick's mysterious cousin by name. Nick spoke of Molly often, but we had never met her.

"Yeah, you, Nick, me, Kay and Molly. It could be fun, like a real birthday," she said.

Real birthday. I wasn't sure they existed. They were like Christmas and Easter and all the other things the kids at school got excited about, but just fell away from us like any other day.

"I don't know where Kay lives," I said. Her face fell a bit, but she went back to cooking.

The smell of burning breakfast roused Lily from her sleep and she joined us, not saying anything, just sitting in the corner and scowling. The older she got, though, the more she resented being there and the harder living with her became.

I began dishing the blackened pancakes onto my plate when the knock at the door startled me. The sound was unfamiliar to us. Ours wasn't the neighborhood for solicitors, and we weren't the family for visitors. I noticed that Menna didn't flinch, but headed over quickly to answer it. Seconds later she closed the door again and Nick appeared in our house.

He looked strange, inside, the house seeming to overwhelm his figure. He was squarely built, standing a full foot above Menna, and yet in our vestibule something about him was so tiny and fragile. Everything about him was more Indian than I had ever noticed—the long dark hair, the black eyes, his nose, his skin, even his tennis shoes seemed to imply that he was different. He looked as though he might have been transposed from the pages of a book into our home.

Inadvertently, I glanced at Lily.

She had never met Nick, nor to my knowledge heard mention of him, and now she stood, her mouth gaping and her eyes wide.

I braced myself for her reaction.

"Good morning," Nick said quietly. His demeanor revealed that he felt the awkwardness the rest of us saw.

"Hey," Menna said, throwing her arms around his neck briefly and returning to the kitchen to busy herself with cooking, as though nothing were out of the ordinary.

"Hi, Max," he said as he followed her into the room, his feet shuffling quietly along the floor.

"Hi," was all I could manage before Lily announced herself.

"Who the hell are you?" she demanded.

He turned to her, his eyes utterly calm and gave her his name.

"Lovely," she said. "You two vagrants have to make friends with the one person in the fucking town lower then you are." She got up and walked out of the kitchen, leaving a wounded silence in her wake.

60

Menna's mouth was hanging open, cheeks flushed, eyes filling with tears. I wondered what she would do, and I got up to silence her fury, to hold her and make her OK, but Nick beat me to it, throwing an arm around her shoulder and pulling her quaking form to him. "It's OK," he said, "she just doesn't understand."

His words only exacerbated Menna's hysteria, and she pulled away from him to follow my sister from the room.

"Damn you Lily," she screamed to the shut door to my sister's room. "You're so sure that everyone else is so low, take a look in a mirror."

The door flew open immediately, Lily standing in the frame blocking the light from behind her. Her eyes were wild and furious. In a second she strode across the room and slapped Menna clean across the face, sending her to her knees. I was beside her in a second, helping her to her feet. By the time she stood, the door to Lily's room slammed again, leaving her and Nick and me to fill a very startled silence.

Nick and I held Menna between us, me covering her mouth and him securing her fists to keep her from provoking more of a fight. The handprint across her face burned angry red and had begun to swell. We ushered her out the door and started towards the hill.

We let her go before we reached the clearing and watched as searing tears fell down her cheeks. She charged ahead of us, leaving Nick and me to stare at her back, quaking with sobs and defiance.

She entered the woods where we always did, between the two magnolia trees. She charged along the dirt that we had, by this time, trampled into a path, past the huge oak tree that stood, twisted and dead, to remind us that we were halfway.

We followed her all the way to the hill and watched her throw her body to the earth. She grasped at the grass with her fingers and ripped it from the ground. She sobbed violently.

We stood back for a while, let her rage on. Finally Nick went to her, touched her back to quiet her, and wrapped his arms around her as she cried.

"I hate her," she claimed.

"I know," he said.

"I'm sorry for what she said."

"I know."

I stood back and watched them, approaching after a few minutes and sitting beside them. Menna pulled away from Nick and sat between us. I looked at her profile for a while, noticing that her eyes were sad like Nick's.

"You didn't bring Molly," she said.

"She wouldn't come," he explained. "She seemed, I don't know, nervous that you guys wouldn't like her."

"Why would she be nervous?" I asked. It seemed odd to me, those that lived behind a formidable chain link fence being scared of us on the other side, on our hill.

"Wouldn't you be nervous, being over there?" he asked me.

The idea seemed absurd. Venturing beyond the hill, behind it, the opposite of the direction from which we came, and walking up to the fence. "I don't know," I said.

He took that response, and met it with silence, staring at Menna's profile and watching the puffy redness around her eyes begin to dissipate.

"I have a present for you," Nick said after a while. "For each of you."

"Why?" I asked.

"For your birthdays."

Menna and I glanced at each other. We had never received any birthday presents before. I don't think either of us knew how to respond, so we both just said, "OK."

Nick first reached into his pocket and pulled out some crumpled pages, which he handed to me. At the top of the first page was scrawled "The Ridge." I said the simple title out loud, slowly, letting the name fall from my tongue. "What's this?" I asked.

"The Ridge is what we call our little town," he said, and I regarded him quizzically. In all the years of living in the town, no one ever called it anything but Over the Fence. Now it had a name. "I asked my grandfather to tell me a story, something about our past. That's it, the story. I thought you would like it."

I glanced down at the pages, brown and torn, crumpled, with writing scrawled across them in massive, cursive loops that were almost illegible. "And he just wrote them down for you?"

"No, he can't write in English, he told me and I wrote it down for you," he told me.

I knew then, somehow, despite my youth, that this was special somehow—sacred. Those words, sloppy and mis-spelled, were suddenly more important to me than anything. I folded them up carefully, thanked Nick, and sat down. I felt the gravity of the pages, this story pulling me to the earth, and wondered how so much had slipped so easily into my pocket, had fit so neatly behind a chain link fence.

"That's so amazing," Menna said, staring at me, knowing the gift was hidden in my pocket.

There was a thick silence as we all considered what Nick had done. He had opened up the door to another world and let me in. I knew from regarding Menna's face that she was intensely jealous of my gift, not just the papers and the story, but the trust Nick must have had to give me a piece of his history.

"I didn't forget you, Menn," he said quietly after a moment, probably seeing her face.

"You didn't?" her voice oozed with hope and anticipation.

"Of course not," he said, reaching into his pocket and handing her something. It was something small, I didn't even see it until she had examined it for a full minute, then held it up to the sunlight.

It was a small piece of leather, with beads surrounding it. Scratched on the leather in the same loopy writing that covered my papers was one word that neither of us recognized. It was clearly not in English.

She stared at it in awe, amazed almost. The gift was small, obviously hand-made, rudimentary, but she stared at it as though it were a diamond.

"What is it?" I asked.

"It's a bracelet," he responded before she could.

"What does it say?" she asked.

Max and Menna

He pronounced the word for her, slowly and articulately. The sound of his native tongue rolling from his mouth was foreign to us, strange. Suddenly he seemed very exotic to us, with these two gifts that showed us a part of life on the other side of the fence.

"What does it mean?" she asked him, her eyes wide as she stared up at him.

Nick looked down at her softly, smiled a little and ran his hand down the side of her cheek. "I'll tell you another day," he promised, smiling wider as their eyes met and her face erupted in happiness.

"Thank you," she said, her tiny voice filled with more gratitude then I have ever heard elsewhere. They stared at each other for a moment, then Menna threw her arms around him. He wrapped his around her and they held each other for a long time.

Menna and I had always shared everything—a room, a face, a life— but on the hill, at that moment . . . that moment was something I knew I could never share. It was theirs, and suddenly I knew I was the one who was foreign. I hugged my knees and waited for the feeling of outside-ness to pass.

I guess it never completely did.

I left the hill without Menna that day, making an excuse of needing to write. I'd left early before, but she had always come with me. This time, she didn't even offer. I knew it wasn't that they didn't want me there, but something in me felt awkward, like I was staring at someone naked, like there was something I wasn't meant to see. I know Menna was far too young at the time to understand—hell, so was I—but Nick knew why I left.

The walk through the woods by myself was strange. I almost got lost, feeling that without Menna I had lost one of my eyes. She knew the trees far better then I, and I meandered for quite a while longer then usual before breaking into the clearing and seeing my house ahead.

A house with no lights on.

Something about that struck me as odd, as darkness was already falling and the kitchen light was almost always on, day or night. However, odd as it seemed, it didn't occur to me to worry. My mother was supposed to be at work, and I was sure Lily must be out, she usually was, especially this early at night.

I walked the rest of the way home, not really dwelling on the darkness, not really worrying until I opened the front door and heard a small, whimpering noise from within.

The TV was on, casting a fuzzy shadow about the room. My mother sat in front of it, her eyes glazed over so that the images from the screen reflected on them. She stared straight ahead. In the darkness I couldn't even tell if she was breathing. Then I looked down and saw the bottle in her hand.

I followed the crying noise to the back of the house and found Lily curled up in a ball in the corner of her room. She was wearing the same t-shirt she had been that morning and nothing else. She was crying softly.

I stood for a while, not quite sure what to do. I wanted to touch her shoulder, see if she was OK, but had no idea how she would react, so instead I breathed her name quietly.

She looked up, revealing blood caked onto her lip, dried from where it had burst from her nose. "Go away, Max," she said after seeing me.

"Lily, are you OK?" I took a step closer to her.

"Get out of here!" she shrieked, startling me. All at once I noticed my mother behind me.

"Oh, so you tell this man to get out, huh?" she spat, saliva flying from her lips. She circled Lily over and over again, darting a foot forward now and then like she would pounce. "You'll tell him, but not that other one, huh? You stupid slut." With the word "slut" she viciously kicked my sister, sending her hip slamming into the wall.

I didn't know what to do, how to react. I wanted more then anything to help my sister, but couldn't for a moment imagine how to stop my mother, so I stood there, dumbfounded, stood there and watched her get kicked twice more, each time yelping a bit, crying harder, biting back words. I stood there.

A hand on my shoulder distracted me. I looked up to see Menna and Nick had also entered the room. Menna glanced at me, bewildered, and then did something I don't understand to this day.

She stepped forward, towards my mother, and ever so gently took her hand. "Come on, Momma," she said, "it's time for bed."

My mother stared down at her, this small, frail girl, and stopped seething for a moment. Menna's tone soothed her, I guess, and she just walked from the room. I turned and watched her go, heard her heading up the stairs, faltering once or twice, slamming into the wall here and there.

When I turned to again regard the scene, Nick was gathering Lily into his arms, Lily who had this morning called him trash and slapped his friend. And still, he picked her up, and she rested her head on his shoulder, leaving red strands of hair and red streaks of blood on his shirt. He carried her into the living room and put her on the couch.

"Menna, washcloth," he said over his shoulder, sending Menna darting into the kitchen to comply. She came back with a wet rag and a bag of ice, placed it gently over Lily's split lip, then dabbed away the blood from her nose.

All the while Lily stared at him as though he were an alien. "Why are you doing this?" she asked finally, moving her face out from behind the ice.

"You're hurt," he said.

She leaned back and closed her eyes, accepting the ice when he handed it to her and covering her face with it.

"Who was here?" I asked finally, amazed by my mother's anger. She was often docile when drunk, and even her fits of rage were short-lived. One punch, one kick, and she would move on. Often she cried. I had never seen her persistently violent before, though suddenly realized where all of Lily's black eyes came from. I guess I had never really questioned all that intensely before.

"Emery," she said quietly.

By now the name was common in conversations with Lily, but we had yet to see a face to associate with it. I knew he lived in town, knew he was older, had his own apartment. Aside from Lily the kids at school talked about him with a sense of awe and terror, though no one could ever say why. He was always with Jimmy Reid, who we always equated with malice.

"Mama walked in and he was here and she hit the roof," Lily said, "and she hit me and he left and she kept hitting me." Tears began to stream down her face. Nick stood back and assumed a place at the back of the room awkwardly.

"I'm going to go now," he said after a moment, and slipped out before any of us had actually heard him.

A few moments later Lily got up off the couch and went to her room, slamming the door behind her, leaving Menna and I to stare at each other in awe, feeling very old for only being fourteen.

Menna

I met Molly a few weeks after our fourteenth birthday. Nick had appeared on our porch suddenly one morning. That summer, Max had been coming with me to the hill more often, but disappearing early. I don't know where he went or why, but after a few minutes there he always seemed uncomfortable and found a reason to leave.

As a result, Nick and I spent most of our time alone together. In the afternoon hours we discussed his plan at length. Nick wanted to move to Maine. He wanted to live along the coast, and work in town during the tourist season. He knew he could make enough money during the summer to spend his winters on the beach thinking.

Nick loved to think. More and more he was telling me what those thoughts were, what rolled around in his head when he sat with his eyes closed on this hill. I'd begun to realize, that summer, how beautiful he was. I wouldn't call him handsome, though outwardly he certainly was. I had come to enjoy listening to his deep voice reverberate as the wind blew his long hair around. His profile was strong, and his face was always slightly sad and slightly whimsical. But he was more than handsome. His face, his hair, his thick shoulders and the warmth of his skin, all of it had begun to make me ache to be near him, but it was his words and his voice that made me want to be with him, that made him beautiful to me in a way I didn't quite understand.

Since our birthday, I had kept the simple bracelet in my pocket always. I was afraid, inexplicably, to put it on. I didn't want it to fall from my wrist as I tore through the trees to get here. I didn't want Lily to see it and question. I didn't want Max to catch me looking at it, tracing the strange word. I wanted it to be mine.

Twice in the weeks that had passed since he gave it to me I had asked him what the word meant. Both times he had smiled as he had when he handed it to me and simply said, "I will tell you another day."

The day I met Molly, it was securely in my pocket, and I moved it about in my hand as Max and I came out of our front door. Nick was sitting there when we stepped out to go to the hill, sitting perfectly still like he might well have been there all night. We paused, and I looked at Max instinctively.

Max had told me, in his terse and guarded way, how weird it made him feel to see Nick at our house. I didn't quite understand it, though more and more, I didn't quite understand Max. Seeing Nick anywhere made me happy and content and comfortable.

"Good morning," I said finally. Nick opened his eyes and turned to see us standing there. He grinned broadly.

"Let's go," he said quickly, then took off towards the woods.

We followed him as best we could, though his zeal carried him along quickly. "I can't wait," he said, smiling over his shoulder occasionally.

The heat made his pace offensive, and Max and I both ached for a chance to catch our breath. We reached the hill very quickly, and, looking up, both instantly noticed a seated figure.

"You're going to meet Molly," Nick said.

So the figure was Nick's cousin Molly, whom he spoke of often, but we had never met. "Cool," Max said, following as Nick began plowing up the hill. I hung back for a moment, suddenly nervous. This was the only other figure of any importance in Nick's life. I suddenly wished I had braided my hair more neatly, or had worn a different shirt. I took a deep breath and followed before they noticed and thought something was strange about my hesitation.

Nick sat next to his cousin and beamed at us while we, standing above them, were introduced. Molly looked somewhat like him, with the same square jaw and large, brown eyes. Her shoulders were more narrow, and there was something more feminine about her mouth and nose. She was strikingly beautiful. "I'm very glad to meet you Molly," I said. I sat a little away from the two of them.

"And I to meet you, too," Molly smiled softly. "Nick rarely talks about anything but the two of you."

Hearing that made me smile broadly. "Really?"

"Yes," she said. "Every time we pray to stones, he mentions you."

My cheeks flushed. Nick, Molly and Max all smiled at the joke, but I felt as though she was mocking me and immediately fell silent.

"Molly is going to college in a couple of weeks," Nick said. He looked at her proudly, and I suddenly found myself just wishing she would go away, though I felt guilty for the thought. "She is very smart," Nick continued.

"Nick," she elbowed him and blushed deeply.

"Max is super smart, too," I said. "He will probably go to Harvard or something. Be a lawyer or something." They all looked at me as I spoke and I suddenly felt self-conscious about my own voice.

"Maybe," Max said. "Menna thinks because she doesn't like school that she isn't smart."

Nick smiled at me in a brief, knowing way, and then turned his attention back to Molly, whose own smile was odd. "I hate school, Menna," she said. Her tone was justified, given that she was four years older, but she seemed so condescending. I looked away.

"What are you going to school for?" Max asked. Any talk of school got him excited. I rolled my eyes.

"A doctor," she said. "I want to become a doctor and go work on a reservation out in Washington or Montana, to help people."

"Help them with what?" I asked, sounding more defensive then I intended to.

Nick looked at me sharply. "When they are sick, Menna. We Indians do get sick."

My face burned with the comment, and the others fell silent. "That isn't what I meant," I said, struggling to my feet and heading down the hill towards the tree. I heard Nick calling after me, but I ignored him and pushed my way through the trees.

I wasn't angry with Nick, though I couldn't figure out why I had needed to flee. My face was red with shame, for I realized he thought I merely regarded him as an Indian, which is seldom something I thought about at all.

I reached in my pocket, felt the bracelet there, and yanked my hand away. I didn't want to be reminded of the gift, of the word I couldn't know because I was stupid or because I didn't understand what it meant to be Indian.

I was nearly home when Nick caught up to me. "Menna, stop!" he called ahead.

I did, though didn't turn to face him. He came up behind me and put his arms around my waist. He pulled me up to him. "I'm sorry," he whispered in my ear. His breath was warm against my skin, and my face flushed again.

"You're sorry I'm stupid," I said. I couldn't push my embarrassment away enough not to fill my voice with anger.

"No one called you stupid," he said, his mouth still close to my ear. "No one thinks you are stupid, and I know you didn't mean that the way it sounded."

"You sure looked like you did," I said, though my embarrassment was fading, replaced by a weird nervousness from being so close to him.

"I'm sorry, I didn't mean it. I'm just nervous. Molly is important to me . . . "

I stepped away. "You don't want me to embarrass you in front of your cousin. I get it. I will go home, and not be in the way."

"Menna," he said sternly. "You are being ridiculous."

I reeled on my heel and stared at him. "I'm ridiculous? Because I don't want to be teased?"

"No," he said. "You're acting ridiculous because you seem to think I would let someone do something to hurt your feelings. That I would hurt your feelings." His voice was hard, and I could see in his face that he was upset.

I stood silently, now more embarrassed by this discussion than I had been by the teasing on the hill. Nick stepped towards me, wrapped his arm around me and hugged me tightly.

I wasn't hugged often as a child. Occasionally Max would hug me. I think my mother might have once. Something about this was different. Nick pressed his hands on my back and pulled me close to him.

"Please, I was just teasing," he said. "Please don't be angry."

Tears came to my eyes, though I certainly didn't know why, and I sobbed openly into his chest. "I'm not angry," I managed, struggling for breath between sobs.

"Then what?"

I stepped back from him and turned away so he wouldn't see my tear-stained face.

"Menna," he grabbed me by the hand and made me look at him. "Molly and I are very close, but so are you and I." He wiped a strand of hair away from my face, leaving a streak of skin that seemed to burn every place he had touched. "I love you guys, Menna, you and Max are very important to me. Don't forget that."

"I . . . we . . . love . . . " I was glad the crying would cover my inability to find the right words. "You're my best friend."

"Come back with me," he said. "Come and get to know my cousin."

"I can't Nick," I said. I had stormed away like a fool. I couldn't go back red-faced and look at them. I couldn't go back feeling as I did after Nick had been so close to me. I couldn't look at him in front of Molly or Max, because I was just sure they would see something in the look that would let them know something I didn't fully understand.

"I want you to," he said calmly.

"I can't," I said again. "Tell her I'm sorry, tell her I'm stupid, I don't care."

He smiled. "She's heard me talk about you enough; she knows that you are stubborn and proud."

I felt anger flood over me, but before I could react, Nick put both hands on my shoulders. "And she knows you are sweet and thoughtful and that you mean a lot to me."

I nodded, and walked away again, feeling the distance between us growing wider and wider.

Chapter Five

*M*ax sits in the parking lot staring at the door to the bar until three different people approach him, asking for some readies. He grows sick of the harassment, and walks in.

The place is called "Rose's" but all of the bartenders are all men. It is strangely full for a Thursday morning. He walks to the nearest stool and orders a beer. The man eyes him. "You lost?"

"No," Max says, then sits down on a torn-up bar stool. "Do I look lost?"

The man shrugs. "You look like someone who quit and stopped here 'cause they didn't realize Vegas is only another ninety miles."

"I came from that direction," Max says. "Well, north of there."

"And you passed on by Sin City, huh?" the man handed him his beer. Max handed him some ones.

"Not much into gambling."

"They have pretty girls in Vegas too," the bartender makes change and sets it on the bar.

"I have a girl; just taking a trip without her right now," Max stares intently at his full glass.

The bartender watches Max, then asks him if he is going to drink the beer or stare at it. Max stares at him. "Just haven't had one in a while," he says, picking it up and gulping it down quickly. He ordered another.

"Must have been a long while," the bartender says.

"You have no idea," Max says, gulping down the second just as quickly.

Netis would be angry, he knows, seeing him drink like this. Since that second night he had known her—a night when they talked until he fell asleep on her couch around dawn—they had never really let alcohol be part of their lives. Like him, she had lost most of her childhood to the alcoholism of her parents. Netis, however, had been the oldest and had raised three brothers as best she could.

"Wasn't easy," she would say when it came up. "But you do what you have to do." She seemed to find it odd that he was confused by this family allegiance. He never explained why, because then he would have to tell her about Menna. That part of his life he had tried so hard to keep away from her. A ringing phone had changed so much so fast.

Max

I felt that year that I was drowning, constantly gasping for air amidst the intense heat. I was fifteen and practically friendless— Menna was gone to me by then, leaving me feeling uncomfortably empty. It had started much earlier, of course, when Nick gave her that bracelet with the unintelligible word scrawled across it. Something in the way they looked at each other as he handed it to her, something about the way she stared at it when no one was around, just told me that the hill was now their world and I was no longer part of it. So I had stopped going there at the end of the previous summer.

The days when she was gone filled me with worry. I had always been there to make sure she was OK and now I felt out of place when I was with her. I knew Nick would protect her. I knew in the way he looked at her that he would never hurt her, but I felt like, in not going there, I was abandoning her even though it was she who had abandoned me.

Not going there meant that I suddenly had no place to go at all, so I stayed home a lot, locked up in the attic, devouring books from the public library, transcribing the stories from my head onto torn-up scrap paper on my old, barely working typewriter. I read two books a day, sometimes more, wrote pages upon pages, and seldom emerged. Menna started calling it my hole, which I knew was probably just her way of saying she was worried about me. Menna usually said things like that in a funny way.

One day in late June, a tattered copy of *Huck Finn* in my hands, I heard my mother walk in the front door. It was around three o'clock, her normal time for knocking off of whatever job it was she had then, so I thought nothing of it, until I heard her begin to bump into things and curse under her breath. She was drunk.

I didn't really think much of her inebriation either, that was certainly nothing new. When she began to mount the stairs to the attic, I began to wonder. Her room was on the second floor, and she seldom climbed any farther up then she had to. I remember her setting foot in the attic less then ten times in all of my childhood.

"Max! Menna!" she bellowed as she neared the top. I stood and went to open the door for her.

"What?"

She stared at the blank space behind me. "Where's your sister?" she demanded.

"She isn't here. What's wrong?"

She ignored my question and continued up the steps, pushed me out of the way and headed towards the center of the room, where she stood for a long time, looking sad and confused. Suddenly, she sat down dramatically and stared at me.

"My father always hated me," she said. "Always, he tried to tell me he didn't, but he was a Southern Baptist minister, and I couldn't never do nothing right in that man's eyes to save my soul."

I had no idea how to respond to this. My mother almost never spoke to me, and never about her past in any way. I just stood and looked at her. She met my eyes, and I could see she was about to cry.

"I know you kids hate me, I know that," she said. "I try not to fuck up all the time, but I just can't do it. It's the way I am. It's what my daddy hated about me so much." She gave a short, burst of laughter that sounded strange coming from her. I tried to remember the last time I had heard her laugh. Nothing came to mind.

"You should have seen that bastard's face when he found out I was pregnant with Lily. He smacked me hard, knocked me backwards down the stairs, then had the nerve to tell me I had to name it after him if it was a boy."

She looked away from me then, to the floor, pulled her legs up to her chest and huddled into a little ball. "So I named her after her father, kind of. His name was Liam. I got the L and the I in there for him. He was gonna marry me when she was born, but got one look at her and went running." She began to cry then, tears streaming down her face as she spoke. "I loved that man, and Lily, she got in the way. Your father, he never gave me nothing but heartache and twins. But Liam, he was something. I still think about him every day."

I didn't want to hear her rant anymore, so I backed up slowly and left. She was still talking as I headed down the stairs. She was up there for hours, and for all I know she talked to me the whole time.

The house felt like water to me then—like it too was trying to drown me. I hit the landing of the second floor and kept going, down to the living room and out the door.

I instinctively started for the library. It was where I spent all the time I couldn't stand being home.

The library was on the farthest corner of town away from the fence. The only black person in town I knew by name was Kay, whose voracious reading and tenacity had now placed her a grade ahead of me. She had penetrating blue eyes and always smelled soft. She had approached me one day at the very beginning of the

75

summer and commenting on my book—*Gulliver's Travels*—which she had loved. We began to talk that day, and every day since that we saw each other at the library.

When I walked in that particular afternoon, fleeing from my mother's desire to vent, Kay was sitting at a table near the door, pouring over *The Dubliners*. I sat down silently across from her and let her keep reading. When she was done, she looked up at me with fat tears in her eyes.

"You OK?" I asked, never having seen her like this before.

"Yes, read this," she said, and pushed a page with a few paragraphs on it towards me. I now know it was the end of the last story—"The Dead"—and it's now one of my favorite pieces of writing.

"It's amazing," I said after skimming it. At the time I wasn't sufficiently moved by the language. Kay noticed and was obviously irritated. She snatched the book back from me and began to read out loud. When she reached a particularly moving line, she became too choked up to finish and closed the book.

"Kay, it's pretty, but damn . . . " I said.

"I know, I know," she replied, smiling, "it's just so beautiful."

A librarian walked past and coughed conspicuously under her breath. This was a daily occurrence to reveal her irritation with our presence. At first I thought it was directed towards me—for being practically the only white person in the library—then towards Kay—for being seen with a white person—but eventually I just assumed it was towards both of us, just for *being*.

Kay rolled her eyes in response to the librarian, and turned her attention to me again. "What you on now?" she asked.

"Just about to finish *Huck Finn*," I said.

The librarian walked back by again, sighing dramatically.

"This shit is getting old," Kay said, loud enough for the woman to hear. Aside from my mother and sister, she was the only girl I had ever heard swear. At first it was shocking, but then I merely began to accept it as part of Kay. "Let's get out of here."

Her suggestion shocked me a bit; I think I might have even flinched. We had never left the library together before.

"And go where?" I asked.

"Anywhere but here," she said, standing and gathering her things as though my response was inconsequential. After a moment of my gawking at her and her suggestion, she placed her hands emphatically on her hips and said, "Well come on."

So I followed her out of the room, not really sure where we would go. We made it as far as the front steps before her confidence began to ebb, her shoulders slumping, her head naturally falling downward. "What now?" she turned and asked me, as though the outside were my realm and my responsibility.

I thought for a moment, then settled on going to see what Nick and Menna were doing. "Follow me," I said.

We walked side-by-side through town, ignoring the stares we got, back past my house, through the woods and to the hills. Of course Menna and Nick were there, this was their realm.

"Hey," we all said uncomfortably as Kay and I marched up the hill.

"This is Kay," I said.

"Hello," Nick said, immediately standing and offering his hand. Menna, who had met my friend before, smiled quietly and we all sat down to continue with what Menna and Nick had been doing before we arrived, which turned out to be absolutely nothing.

"This is what you folks do all day, every day?" Kay asked after a while.

"No, sometimes we wander through the woods," Menna said.

"Ah, anything else?" she asked.

"Not really," we admitted.

"Well how 'bout swimming? Let's go swimming," she suggested.

Doing something else—the concept seemed so foreign to us. But we agreed to give it a try and followed Kay as she knowingly guided us to the stream by her house. The area was well-visible from the road, but there weren't any houses in visual range.

We all jumped in the water, clothes and all, and begin to swim about and splash like mad.

"Good idea, Kay," Menna said after a while. Her drenched hair hung about her in long, straggly locks. She and Nick would slide themselves under water and come up with their hair the same.

"Yeah, my dad brings us out here sometimes at night and we go swimming," Kay explained with a large smile.

"Your dad lives with you?" Menna asked, a little surprised.

"Yeah, of course," Kay said.

"What's he like?" Menna asked, swimming over to stand near Kay.

"He's pretty cool," Kay said. "He reads to me and stuff. Says I better be the first in my family to go to college."

"College," Nick uttered.

Menna assumed a pensive look. "I bet my father would want me to go to college, too," she said quietly, sadly, then dove underwater and swam further out then she had before.

Nick turned and looked at me strangely, as did Kay. "I didn't think you knew your father," Kay said.

"We don't," I explained, "but I think Menna likes to wish we did a lot more then she lets on."

Later several of Kay's friends slid their bodies into the water and began to swim with us. We were quite an eclectic looking group, but nobody really noticed. We just swam, letting the water wash the heat of the summer day and the dirt of the town from our bodies.

The sun was beginning to fade when a sharp, barking voice drew our attention from the water. "Hey, all of you hoodlums, out of there," a man called from the road. We looked up to find a policeman standing beside his car, hands on hips and his lips turned into a snarl.

"We ain't hurting nobody," one of Kay's friends screeched at the man.

"That don't matter none," the cop replied, "you ain't supposed to be swimming here, now get out."

We complied, marching out of the water, one by one, all feeling very small and angry that our fun had been interrupted.

As the officer drove off, Kay and her friends started home and Menna, Nick and I started towards our end of town. "He didn't have to call us hoodlums," Menna complained as we walked on. Her pride seemed hurt, but I guess this was nothing new with Menna.

"We weren't doing nothing wrong," I added.

"We just look wrong," Nick said.

His words were followed with silence, as they were strange and it took us some time to understand. Kay and her friends were black, Nick Indian, Menna and I white. We didn't look *right* at all.

We parted ways and Menna and I went home. Kay looked at me strangely before she left, a strange look that I could not wash from my mind. It plagued me the whole way home, trying to figure out what it had meant. She looked sad, definitely, but something else, too. Something softer, something less tangible. Defeated perhaps. Betrayed, perhaps. Wise, perhaps.

We stopped at the street and said a quick good-bye to Nick before climbing the steps to our house, though. There was a man on my porch, sitting next to Lily. He was facing her, holding her face in her hands.

"Who's that?" I asked Menna, who stared at him in a quiet, knowing fashion.

"Emery," she said.

"Should we go in?" I asked.

"Why not? We live here," she declared, her voice firm. But, as she walked up the steps, her stride was not so confident. The closer we got to the porch, the slower and more gingerly she began to walk.

Lily looked up sharply when we walked onto the porch. It was a strange look she gave us—not her normal angry gaze, but rather a look of something all together different, but still rather negative. Something like fear.

"What the hell do you two want?" she asked. When I heard her voice, a bit higher than usual, quavering ever so slightly, I knew for a fact that she was afraid.

"We're just going inside," Menna said. She stood with defiance, but her voice sounded the same as Lily's.

They began to bicker, Lily telling her to watch her mouth, Menna retorting that Lily wasn't her mother; I ignored them, though, and for the first time got a good look at Emery.

He was tall, even seated. He had blond hair that hung to his shoulders in a frenzied way. The length didn't seem intentional, merely overlooked, from the way it shone with grease and dirt. His face was equally as disheveled, with a few days of beard sprouting. His eyes were set far back into his head, and were surprisingly blue, so much so that from several feet away I could clearly detect their color.

His hands were filthy, as were his clothes, smeared with stains of varying color and age. His fingernails seemed to be almost painted with soot.

"Hey, kid," his words, thick with the sound of the South, broke me of my observation.

I looked up and met his eyes, but didn't say anything. Lily turned quickly from her argument with Menna to watch him. "What the hell you looking at?" he demanded. He sat perfectly still as he said it, but despite his calmness it seemed as though he might spring from the bench and pounce at any second.

"Sorry," I mumbled before Menna pulled me into the house.

We closed the door behind us an instantly headed upstairs. My mother wasn't home, or was somewhere out of view if she was. Once we reached the attic, we closed and locked the door and sat in silence, both wondering what to make of the day.

"I don't understand, Max," Menna said after a long silence.

"I don't either," though she hadn't specified, merely by looking at her, I knew that she meant all of it. Being called hoodlums, Lily's attachment to this dirty, angry man, all of it was incomprehensible to her.

Kay's expression again surfaced in my mind, and I rolled it back and forth, over and over. Finally, the expression tickled my feet and I stood.

"I gotta go," I said, striding towards the door.

"Max, where are you going?" she asked, alarmed.

"I have to go, I need to talk to Kay," I said.

"To Kay's . . . you don't know where she lives," she pointed out.

"She lives near the library," I explained.

"Do you want me to go?" she asked.

I thought for a moment, knowing all along the answer was no. When I told my sister that, her face fell, but she nodded, somehow understanding.

Menna

I guess it was the very first day of that summer, lying on the hill, that I noticed how Nick had changed. His hair had grown long, so long he kept it tied back, always. His shoulders were broad now, and he was tall and fully built. His features were carved out more intricately now, not the awkward prominent face he had worn since childhood, but the face of a man. Sometimes a very old man.

He had been eerily silent for the last few weeks. Normally he was not as chatty as I was, but he always at least had something to say in response to me. Though, at that point in time all I could seem to talk about was how my mother was gone. "Maybe she's off to find my father," I said once, right before school let out. Nick was the only living person who knew how I ached to know who my father was, and even he never heard of the dreams that I would wake up one day and find a strange, but familiar looking man leaning over me—a strange man who would gather me up in his arms and carry me far away from this place.

"My mother never goes anywhere," he said in response to me, beginning his unusual tour of silence.

So that day in July when he looked determinedly to me and said, "Come on," I was taken by surprise.

"Where are we going?" I asked as I stood quickly and struggled to keep up with his gaping stride as he headed down the hill and into the woods.

"There is someone I want you to meet," he explained.

I followed him silently through the woods, this time the other way, back towards the fence. I followed him right up to the gates and paused as he entered and beckoned for me to do the same.

"You want me to meet someone here?" I asked, feeling somehow that it would be wrong for me to go in.

"Yes," he said, standing patiently aside and waiting for me to follow.

"Am I, I mean, is it OK if I . . . " I couldn't find any words that didn't sound insulting, so I just said it. "Can I go in there if I'm not Indian?"

He laughed at me then, the way he laughed at me the day we met. "Yes, it's just land, Menn, we will not pray to the stones and ask them to strike you dead for entering."

I knew he was mocking me, and felt that I should be angry, but being here, so near to the opening of the fence I couldn't feel much but nervous. I put my fury on reserve. Nick was there, though, and that made the fear lessen. He took my hand and pulled me through the entrance.

We walked, hand in hand, for what seemed an eternity. There were small houses all around, much smaller than mine, all ramshackle and dilapidated. Here and there people stood in doorways and watched us passively, other stared at windows, but the whole area seemed plagued with a dead calm. Relief washed over me when we passed a group of men playing basketball off in a field. They ran and laughed and kidded each other, and added signs of life to the sweltering world I was treading to.

Nick walked on quickly, staring straight ahead as though he didn't notice anything that was going on around us, until we reached a small, worn-down house. He turned and said to me softly. "This is my house."

We walked into the stifling living room. It looked much like any other living room to me, small and cramped, torn furniture, empty bottles on the table. There were no lights, I noticed, not even a lamp or anything that would illuminate this room in darkness. The room was empty of people, for which I was extremely grateful. I couldn't imagine who he wanted me to meet, but the prospect seemed terrifying. My heart jumped and I quietly thanked God whoever it was wasn't home.

"Hold on," he said, letting go of my hand and leaving me to stand desperately alone in the center of the room. My hope quickly deflated.

I looked around again. There were no pictures on the walls, and the floor was dirt, covered with a small carpet. I stepped forward and sat on the couch, which was itchy and moist. I tried to ignore theses sensations as they plagued my skin, but could not. I shifted positions, pulling the bottom of my denim shorts down to cover more of my legs. This didn't help either, so I got up. It was then that I noticed the activity in the corner of the couch—a small colony of roaches crawling up and down the arm, then back underneath the cushions.

I gagged reflexively as Nick came walking back into the room, leading a small woman by the arms. She wasn't really all that much shorter than he was, but slumped over, making her look ultimately very tiny. What immediately struck me about her was that she could have been amazingly beautiful. She didn't look all together Indian, not as much as Nick did, but seemed to have borrowed the most desirable traits from that race and mixed them with those from another. Her hair was dark like his, but interrupted with streaks of red and thick, unruly waves. Her skin was light, almost as light as mine, which made her black eyes striking. They might have shone that day, had they not been so glazed over.

She took one look at me and plopped defiantly on the couch, yanking her arm away from Nick.

"Hello," she said to me, the word slow and lazy. She leaned over, picked up an empty bottle and flipped it upside down over her mouth. A drop fell out, hit her tongue, and she swallowed, closing her eyes.

"Hi, I'm Menna," I managed to say, stepping forward and holding out my hand.

"Hello," she said again, then leaned back and closed her eyes. Her face was very much like Nick's, strong and sure, and her hair also long like his.

"This is my mother, Menna," Nick said uncomfortably staring at her. After a full minute she made no further movement and Nick ushered me out of the house.

The way back to the fence looked different than the way in there. I guess since this was my second look at these houses, the quiet faces and empty doorways, they seemed so much more familiar.

We followed the trail back to the hill in almost absolute silence. We had almost reached the clearing when I realized he was crying and grabbed his arm, trying to get him to face me. He wouldn't, but instead leaned against a tree, covering his face.

"I'm sorry," he said, "I didn't know she'd be like that, she wasn't when I left this morning, she normally isn't, it's just that. . ."

"What?" I asked, putting my arm softly around his waist and holding him as he cried.

He turned to face me, and I wondered if I should step back—we were mere inches apart. Being this close to him, for some reason, was making my face burn, my stomach jump. It was an odd feeling at that particular moment. We had been close before, many times, hugging, wrestling, just sitting with our arms around each other. Now his hurt hung thick in the air, and the memory of our moment after meeting Molly last summer sprung to mind.

But I didn't step back, but remained in front of him, almost a full foot shorter then he, and staring into his teary brown eyes as he spoke.

"My father is missing," he said simply.

"What do you mean, 'missing'?"

"He went three nights ago, drinking with friends, and hasn't been back yet," he said. "He's stayed out all night before, but this is a new one. My mother has a 'hunch,' said she knows he's dead."

Nick's father had only ever been mentioned in passing to me. The very concept was foreign to me—Max was the only man in my home—so I couldn't begin to understand what was happening in Nick right now. Somehow, strangely enough, I envied him for having a face to attach to his missing father.

So I simply said, "I'm sorry."

"That's the thing," he said, stepping past me. His hand brushed my arm as he did. "I'm not."

"You don't think he's dead?" I asked, a little shocked by his coolness.

"I don't know, he could be, it wouldn't matter," he said. His back was to me, and his voice shook as he spoke. I had never heard him talk like this before; he seemed so cold and callus.

"Nick, he's your father. You should care."

He spun to face me. "How would you know?"

"I wouldn't," I admitted through clenched teeth, my nails biting into my palms. I didn't know if I wanted to cry, or hit him. I stared at the ground, found a crumpled oak leaf at my foot, toyed with it with my big toe, which protruded from a hole in my worn, too small tennis shoes.

"Oh God, Menna, I'm sorry," he said a moment later. "I didn't mean that."

"Fine," I replied. My head was clouding over, so I stared intently at my oak leaf, refusing to look at him. I edged it first this way with my toe, then that, flattening it, then crumpling it again.

"That was an awful thing to say," he admitted, taking a step closer to me, "I didn't mean to hurt your feelings."

"Oh, I'm sure. You don't care about your own father enough to be sad that he's dead, why the hell would you care about hurting me," I said, my fingernails nearly drawing blood from my palms as I clenched my fingers. He leaned over and picked up the leaf, as though removing the distraction would force me to look at him.

I looked up, past him, over his shoulder at a large, gnarled tree.

"It's not that I'm not sad he might be dead," he said quietly. "It's just that if he is, I'd be happy for him. That would mean he got out."

I released the tight fists I had been holding onto so eagerly and looked away from the gnarled tree to his contorted face. I had never seen him look so sad before, so helpless, so small. I stepped into him and put my arms around him softly.

"I needed you to meet my mother," he said, "I needed you to see why I . . . how I could be happy for him . . . "

"I understand," I said, burying my face in his chest. He smelled clean. I could hear his voice reverberating as he spoke, the muscles flex and tense under the smooth fabric of his tee-shirt. It felt cool and soft below my face, which was burning from being so close to him.

"And Menna," he added, "please, never ever think that I don't care about you." He began to talk quickly. "Some days, you're all I care about—you and getting out of here."

His arms tightened around me. I inhaled deeply, smelling the clean smell of him, listening to the air moving in and out of his lungs. After a moment, I could hardly breathe, so I took half a step back to give myself some air but tried not to let go or let him know what I was doing. Nick noticed, however, and pushed me away slightly. I looked down at my feet, across from his feet. A second later I felt his fingers on my chin.

He forced my chin upward until our eyes met. He lowered his face to mine until his mouth was full on my own.

Kissing was one of those things that girls whispered about during class, or that I watched through the fuzz on our TV screen. I was lost, not knowing what to do. Somewhere, deep in my abdomen something went *pop* like the small fireworks the rich kids had on the Fourth of July, and everything at once felt strange, and new, and wonderful. The softness of his mouth on mine, the warmth, all of it made me light-headed and dizzy.

"I'm sorry," Nick said, breaking from me abruptly.

"Why?" I asked.

"I shouldn't have done that. It was wrong," he stammered. "I just . . . "

"Nick," I said quietly, "it's OK."

He stopped fumbling for words and met my eyes again, smiling softly as he did. We might have stood staring at each other for hours for all I know, but it felt like everything else disappeared but him and me and the few trees that surrounded us. I ached, hurt desperately, wanting nothing more than for him to kiss me again. But finally, he simply said, "You're my best friend, Menna."

"I know," was all I could think to say, and he smiled, and wound his arms around my waist.

"Was it OK enough that I can do it again?" he said quietly.

I smiled more broadly then I intended, and he kissed me again. His fingers moved up my back, into my hair, and onto my face. I kissed him back, faintly worried that I was doing something wrong, that he was inwardly laughing at my lack of knowledge. But he only persisted. Somehow, after a few moments, I was clinging to him with a terrified feeling that he might stop. His mouth moved from my lips to my neck, my fingers running through his hair.

As my breath grew ragged and rushed and I found myself leaning into him without meaning to, he stepped back and pulled away from me. He looked at the ground and I could see his shoulders heaving as mine were. He flushed as he looked up at me.

"I'm sorry, I got carried away."

I stepped towards him and put my hand on the side of his face. "Please stop apologizing. I . . . this . . . I mean, I want . . . " I stammered, suddenly not able to remember any of the words I needed. Nick smiled knowingly, and kissed my forehead.

"Walk with me?" he asked, offering me his hand, which I took, and we began to wander through the woods together.

I was wondering why Nick had kissed me, why he had kept saying he was sorry, if he would do it again on another day that wasn't so full of sadness. Not knowing what it had meant, if anything, and if I was supposed to act differently was gnawing at me.

I had seen very little of this part of the woods. Anything that lay between my house and the hill was common knowledge to me, more familiar than my own face. I was on the other side of the hill, now though, between it and the fence.

"How do you know so much about these woods?" I asked, struggling to keep up with him as we walked along a small path.

"I come and walk around here a lot," he explained, "at night sometimes I'll just find a tree out here and think."

"You come here at night, by yourself?" The trees looked large and frightening to me during the day—I couldn't imagine them at night.

He stopped at this question, turning to face me. "When I was little my brother used to beat up on me a lot," he explained. "We shared a room, and he would come in late at night sometimes and just start punching me while I lay in my bed. So, I never let myself fall asleep there, and whenever I heard him coming, I would climb out the window and run over here, find a tree and curl up against it to sleep."

"You sleep out here?" I asked, amazed.

"Not so much anymore," he said, "but I used to nearly every night."

"Did your brother move out?" I asked.

"No, he died," Nick said simply, as though it didn't really matter. "Ran our truck right into a tree."

"What?" I stopped and forced him to look at me.

"Menna, it happened a long time ago, I don't think about it much," he said, though his face betrayed his lie. "I was never home when he was anyway, I was always here."

"Didn't anyone ever notice you were gone?"

He smiled. "Would anyone notice if you were?"

The statement startled me. I thought about it for quite a while, wondering if my mother would even notice my absence, if Lily would give it more than a passing thought. "Just Max."

"Right, and I don't have a Max," he explained. "My cousin misses me sometimes, but she understands."

That statement seemed irrevocably sad to me. My life was far from perfect, and my brother was sometimes annoying, but as far back as I could remember, I'd always had him. He'd always been there at night if I had a nightmare to hold my hand while I fell back asleep. For a moment his absence seemed immense, like it might swallow me, but then I squeezed Nick's hand, and he touched my cheek very gently, and the feeling went away. When he leaned over and kissed me again, it became a distant memory. Any guilt that I might have felt for not missing my brother, for leaving him behind, was swallowed by the feelings that surged through me now.

"Oh, I have to show you this," Nick said quickly, and darted off in another direction, yanking me behind him.

"What?" I asked.

"A little farther out here there is this old abandoned house," he said. "It's really weird. It's all locked up, you can't get inside or anything, but it's still kind of neat."

I ran along behind Nick, my short legs struggling to keep up with his long strides. After a long while we cleared through the trees and I saw a tiny, dilapidated cottage in front of us.

The building was small, covered with growth from where the brush was attacking. "There's a huge window on the other side, and you can see in. There are still paintings on the walls and everything."

He pulled me around to the other side, which was slow going because of all the plants and roots and debris that surrounded the base of the house.

"Why is it abandoned?" I asked, "I mean, who would leave without taking their pictures off the walls or anything?"

"I don't know," he said. "It's really kind of creepy if you think about it."

I didn't want to think about it. I found it strange that Nick often came here on his own, set foot in these woods at night. I found myself worrying about him, wanting to protect him, which seemed odd, tiny me worrying about such a huge man.

"Shhh," Nick said suddenly. We were looking around the corner to where the large window he spoke of must have been. We could hear soft sounds coming from the inside, like someone sighing deeply over and over.

We tiptoed over to the window, crouched down and looked inside. There were two figures on the floor, one on top of the other. I looked closer and saw that it was Lily, only her head and fiery red hair protruding from underneath the body that loomed over her, but said nothing.

The strange noises were coming from her. The man on her rocked up and down, and with each upward movement she would gasp slightly. Her face was contorted in pain, her eyes closed. Nick and I stood watching, not really knowing what to do.

The man spoke suddenly, apparently catching Lily, and us, off-guard. Lily snapped to look at him, her eyes flying open, and Nick and I crouched out of sight. I couldn't hear what was said, but his voice sounded thick and angry.

"No, of course not," Lily said, her voice loud and afraid. Her words were followed by a harsh slap and she cried out slightly.

Nick instinctively moved to stand up. I wondered if he was thinking to fly to her rescue, but I grabbed his arm, knowing that Emery, who I could only assume was the man with Lily, was someone to be avoided.

I pulled Nick's arm, and we darted away through the trees. I walked ahead, tugging at my lip.

"You okay?" he asked from behind.

"Why wouldn't I be?" I asked. I really didn't know what about the scene we had just witnessed upset me, only that it filled me with a strange sorrow, and worry.

"Your sister, Emery . . . " he said.

"You know Emery?"

He nodded gravely. "Everyone in the Ridge knows who Emery is," he explained. "The mayor's nephew. He and Jimmy Reid are always coming across the fence looking for trouble."

Jimmy Reid was the mayor's son, and quite infamous for his exploits throughout town. Emery was equally so, although his exploits somehow remained more eerily private. Jimmy Reid was the type to get caught shoplifting and laugh about it. Emery was who everyone whispered about when someone's cat went missing.

"Why would anyone do that?" I asked him. I thought of the pain on Lily's face, of Emery above her.

"Hang out with Emery?" he asked.

"No, have... do what they are doing . . . ," I said.

He smiled at me. "Sometimes, it's a good thing." As he said it, I imagined him leaning over me, feeling him *that* close. I was sure I began to blush and wasn't able to look at him.

"It didn't look like a very good thing," I said.

Again, Nick put his arms around me. "I'll ask you again in a couple of years if you feel that way still." I wasn't able to feel that way now, his arms around me. Intuitively, I believed sex to be gross. What the teachers taught in school, the mumblings of the ladies in town, what I had just seen happening to Lily—all of this told me that sex was disgusting and immoral. Yet, pressed up against Nick, suddenly every part of my was alive and thinking of nothing else.

"Have you ever done it?" I stepped back from him, imagining, suddenly, him leaning over someone else. An angry knot formed in my stomach, but all I was able to feel was concern.

"Had sex?"

"Yes, had sex," I said.

He half smiled, took my hand and began walking again, leaving me answerless.

Chapter Six

*M*enna notices that Cole is merely playing with her food. "You better eat now," she tells her. "We aren't stopping for at least another three hours and there are no snacks in the car."

"I'm tired," Cole says, reaching for her soda.

"That's your second already—how many pee breaks do you think we'll be making? I can't believe you're drinking soda this early in the morning anyway," Menna says.

Cole shrinks back from the glass and picks up her fork. "It's not morning," Cole reminds her eerily. She forces a bite of grits into her mouth. "Menna, these suck."

"Watch your mouth," Menna retorts without thinking, then softens her tone a bit. "You like oatmeal, these aren't so different."

"Oatmeal has some taste, these things taste like plywood. Can't I have a bagel?" Cole asks.

"They don't serve bagels here."

"What kind of place doesn't serve bagels for breakfast?" Cole looks around in awe, like she has never seen a diner before.

"Baby, we aren't in New York anymore. This is the South, people eat grits and bacon, not bagels," Menna explains, then flags the waitress down and asks for some toast. "I guess this is what I get for never taking you out of upstate."

Cole smiles slightly, then bites her lip the way she does when she is contemplating something.

"Spit it out," Menna says smiling, reading the girl's face easily.

"Did he eat grits?" she asks.

"I suppose, though he was more a fan of sweet potato pancakes," Menna says, reaching for a newspaper and hoping the conversation is over.

"Who makes pancakes out of potatoes?" Cole asks in disgust.

"People who don't complain quite as much as you do," Menna says, and sticks her tongue out. Cole laughs. The waitress brings toast and jam, and the girl digs into it. Menna opens a newspaper in hopes that Cole won't notice her scarcely touched plate.

Silence prevails for a moment, then the girl lifts up the bottom of the newspaper and peeks at Menna. "You're yelling at me, and you haven't eaten a thing."

A steaming plate of biscuits and gravy looks up innocently. "Guess I wasn't as hungry as I thought."

Cole sighs dramatically. "Looking at that would make me lose my appetite."

Menna laughs despite herself and spoons some of the girl's grits into her mouth. "I don't know how you can not like these."

Cole says nothing for a long moment, then, "What's my uncle like?"

"Me, only smarter . . . quieter," Menna says absently, folding up the paper and digging in her purse for some bills.

"If you're twins, don't you miss him?"

"Yes, I do," Menna says, engaging Cole's stare. "I guess sometimes you miss so many people so much that they all kind of blend together and you forget about it."

"You miss *him* more then you miss your brother, don't you?" Cole asks. "Is that why you don't like to talk about him?"

"You know, you are just like your uncle. Full of questions. Now do you want to get out of here or sit around and chat all day?"

"Let's go and chat all day in the car," Cole says.

She is sitting in the car by the time Menna is finished paying the bill. She tugs at her lip as Menna fastens her seatbelt.

"Colie," Menna says, poking her in the side.

The girl pushes her hand away and retreats farther onto the other side of the car. "Cole," Menna says sternly, and she turns to face her. "What?"

"I'm scared," Cole says.

"Of what?"

"Of meeting my uncle. Of seeing your home. I don't know why there are so many things you won't tell me," she says. Fat tears fall from her eyes and hit the vinyl upholstery with a resonant plopping sound.

Menna smiles slightly. "You are too full of worry for such a little person." She slides over the bucket seat and hugs the girl close to her. "Your uncle will love you, and you will love him. And I've been wrong to never tell you who you are before, where you come from. Max should be a part of your life because he is really, really important to me."

"So why haven't we ever seen him before?" Cole asks.

"Because I wasn't ready to tell you about this life," Menna says. "And there are a lot of things about my past with Max that I didn't want to think about." *And,* she thinks, *because I never had to.*

Cole nods and wipes the tears from her face. "Like *him?*" She asks. Her voice always had a different inflection when she was talking about Nick, though she never said his name. Menna was glad for it.

"I think about him every day," Menna says, and slides back over and starts the car absently. She notices the girl, who suddenly seems so small, staring at her shaking hands.

Max

The trouble was brewing long before that July. Menna and I had just turned sixteen. Lily, twenty-two, still haunted the doorways with her sullen, angry jibes. I know now, remembering, that the possibility had always been there, we had just shut it out, on our little hill.

Emery was more of a fixture now; we would find him on the porch at night when Menna and I came home—her from the hill and from Nick, and me from the library or wherever I had been with Kay. The way he looked at us, it was almost as though he could smell the presence of *different* on us.

"The way you kids run wild, that's a damn shame," he muttered once as we headed into the house. Lily passed us, going out. None of us responded, not knowing what to say.

I honestly don't know if any of it was my fault. Maybe Emery saw me with Kay, felt that it was somehow wrong, that he needed to fix it. Then again, maybe he and Jimmy were just bored that day.

May was stifling hot that year, carrying us into a June that was unrelenting and brutal. On the last day of school, Kay and I got off the bus together, and as Menna immediately headed for the hill, I walked her halfway home. She chatted anxiously about upcoming college visits—Kay was starting early—and her plans to go shopping with her mom.

"You're talking a mile a minute," I said finally, and she grinned.

"And you're just moving as slow as ever," she shot back.

"It's too hot to talk fast," I said.

She grinned even more. "Never too hot to talk fast."

We said our good-byes and I headed home. I assumed I would see Kay again the next day at the library, but when I got there, she wasn't waiting for me. So, I found a book and a table and sat to wait for her.

The librarian moved by me some time later, about the time I was beginning to realize that I would spend the day alone, and saw me. A sad look spread over her face as she sat next to me. "Honey," she said, "did anyone tell you about your friend?"

I didn't answer, but looked at her strangely. With this expression, this pity and compassion, she looked so different from the woman who had sneered at us for the past few summers.

She took my silence as an invitation to continue. "She had an accident last night, honey, she's resting at home."Apparently feeling that this was enough information, she got up and walked away. I felt several other odd stares as I moved out of the library.

I knew the way to Kay's house, though I had never been inside. I hesitated at the door, but made myself knock.

A moment later, Kay's father answered. He looked tired and angry. Though he was a tall man, at least eight inches taller than I, he somehow seemed small as he led me wordlessly inside.

Kay was sitting on the couch, her arm in a cast, cuts across her arms and chest, and one eye nearly swollen shut. She tried to grin, but then grimaced as a cracked lip protested. "Hey Max," she said. "How was the library?"

"What the hell happened to you?" I asked in a whisper, as her dad left the room.

Her face grew still. She closed her eyes and leaned her head back on the couch. "Jimmy Reid," was all she said.

"Why?" I asked.

"No reason, I guess. I ran into him on the way home, and he just started hitting me," she said.

I stared at her in silence and disbelief. The mayor's son, who always seemed just a little bit scary to me for inexplicable reasons, now grew stunningly big in my mind. He was huge, with his demented smile and uneasy laugh, and filled my brain instantly.

"What did the police say?" I asked when I found my voice.

She laughed a bit, and sat up to look at me. She grew very serious before saying, "The police said there was no evidence that it was him."

"What?" I asked, shocked. I knew that the stores where he stole didn't press charges, that he never seemed to get in trouble for disrupting town events, or for fights at school. But this, Kay's battered face . . .

"Three people saw it," she continued. "Two of them stopped him after I was on the ground. They said it wasn't enough evidence."

"How can they . . . they can't . . . " I began to stammer. I knew what unfair felt like, having felt it so much for so long, but this was even beyond my scope of understanding. This was wrong.

"He's the mayor's son," she said simply. "And we're just a bunch of Negros that claim he beat up a girl with no provocation or cause."

"Kay," I said, "I am so sorry."

"I know, Max," she said, "and thank you. I got him a few times, too." She smiled a bit.

"Kay, I just don't understand how they can do this," I said. "They" was him, the mayor, the police. "They" was my mother, my absent father, my sister, Emery, the librarian, and so many others.

"I don't know, and I know how you feel," she said. "But now I want you to go." She looked so tired and so angry, so I left. I went home to our empty room because, of course, Menna was at the hill.

I saw so much less of my sister that June, less even than the summer before. She never talked about Nick, about what they did, how he was, and their time on the hill. And yet, at some point, and I don't really even know when, I had suddenly become unwelcome in their world.

Menna still loved me. We still slept on the attic floor, talked into the night. I still needed her voice at the end of the day, but our lives had split and splintered and Nick was her world. I had told her about Kay, and she had put her hand softly on my shoulder, worry clouding her face, but had still been gone the next morning when I woke up.

Right before the Fourth of July, Kay's family left, I guess the anger they all felt when walking through town drove them out. I took a little enjoyment, though, when I saw Jimmy Reid a few days prior and noticed that he had a black eye. Then the library closed due to excessive heat. I found myself alone in the world, no books, no friends, and my sister's life far away from mine.

I had tried to make due, staying at home, re-reading my stories, finishing all of the books on the twelfth-grade reading list that I had taken out before the library's closing, but soon boredom overtook me. At one in the afternoon on that Wednesday, a few days before the planned town carnival, I decided to see just how unwelcome I was with Nick and Menna.

I nearly got lost venturing through the woods to our hill, to *their* hill, since I hadn't been in a year or two. Many times, as I wound through the woods, I considered turning around and going back. I grew more and more nervous as I got closer, wondering if I would be accepted there.

I finally managed to find my way. I stepped into the clearing at its foot and saw them there, lying together.

They weren't speaking, weren't even looking at each other. Nick was on his back, his arm around Menna, who was curled up at his side. Their free hands were tangled together. They both were staring up into the sky.

I had known before then, though it had never been confirmed, that there was more than a friendship between them. I had no confirmation now, I realized, but something about them seemed so comfortable, so natural. I stepped out of the clearing so they wouldn't see me, intending to walk away and leave them to each other, but something made me stop and stare.

I had never seen people together like this before. I had seen Lily and Emery kissing on the porch. I had seen my mother and her boyfriends in their cars out the attic window from time to time. Those interactions weren't like this, they weren't so easy with each other. Nick and Menna. At this moment, I almost felt as though I were staring at them naked, for the way they touched each other was so intimate.

As I stood there, Menna rolled onto her stomach, her arm laid across his chest. Nick laughed at something she said, put his hand behind her head, and pulled her face close to his.

I instinctively retreated into the woods, breaking a branch as I did. I ducked back below the trees.

I saw Nick sit up, and then Menna after him. He looked in the direction of where I stood, suddenly alert. Menna glanced my way as well, but only for a moment before touching his face and pulling it towards her. He kissed her then, and they fell backwards onto the ground, intertwined again.

I had kissed Kay once. On the way home from the library we had stopped for an ice cream. She ate hers quickly, but still some melted down her chin. Without thinking, I had reached to wipe it away, and then without considering it at all, had leaned forward and kissed her.

She had frozen then, hands at her sides, mouth slack. "Max," she whispered, stepping back, "we're in the middle of town and we really shouldn't let people see that."

Nothing about it seemed like this, like Menna and Nick. I tore back through the woods on my way home. I know that I had known, somehow without being told, what their relationship had become. I had known by the quiet contentment that had washed over Menna over the past months, they way she seemed milder, less quick to anger. I occasionally caught her smiling and asked why, but she always pointed to a funny show she was thinking of, a cartoon she had just read.

My sister was happy and was working as hard as she could to keep me from seeing it. My sister was no longer my companion, no longer my responsibility. I felt, suddenly, very alone.

When Menna crept home that night, I pretended to be asleep. I was on the far side of the attic away from her, but she knew without saying a word that I was wide awake.

"It was you we heard in the woods today, wasn't it?" she asked.

"Yes," I said quietly, not sure why I wanted to lie but having to force the truth.

"Oh," was all she could reply.

"How long have you two been . . . " I asked, my voice trailing off as I realized that I had no idea what to call whatever they were.

"Since last summer," she said.

"Oh."

"It's not what you think, Max," she said quickly.

"And what do I think?"

"You think we're like Lily and Emery and we . . . "

"I don't think that." I said, hoping that this conversation was over.

"We aren't," she pressed on. "We don't, I mean . . . we haven't," it was odd to hear this embarrassment in her normally proud voice. "We're leaving."

I sat up without thinking about it. "When?"

"Next summer, after I graduate. We're going to go to Maine. Nick wants to find work, and I am going to get a job, and we're getting away from here together," she explained.

I was suddenly furious without fully knowing why. She had every right to leave, hell, I had thought of it, dreamt of it myself on so many occasions, but I had always silently imagined her with me. And now, she was going without me. The words fell from my mouth before I could stop them. "I'm sure he would say anything to get you to fuck him."

Menna sucked her breath in angrily, but a few seconds passed before she responded. "No one is 'fucking' me, Max. Nick hasn't even tried. It's not about that. I am *not* Lily."

"I know, I'm sorry."

"I love him, Max."

"I know." *And I'm sorry.*

The air between us was thick, humid, and tense. Finally, I rolled to my side. "Will you two come to the Fourth of July carnival with me?"

She laughed a little. "We've never gone to that stupid thing before."

"I know. Let's go. This will be your last fourth here. Spend it with me, the both of you."

I could hear the smile in her voice. "OK."

"Goodnight," I said, smiling myself and rolling over.

"Max, come north with us."

I sat up again. "What am I supposed to do in Maine?" I demanded.

"Apply for college. Write. What are you planning on doing here?"

I left her question hanging in the air because I had no answer.

Menna

Honestly, I didn't want to go. Max asked that we go to the carnival, and I agreed, and I asked Nick to meet us at our house and go with us. He had, of course, agreed, though I could tell in the momentary pause before he'd answered me that he didn't want to, either.

But, I felt like I owed this to my brother, who I had quickly removed from a place of prominence in my life as Nick became the central figure. I felt as though I had betrayed Max, but even the guilt wasn't enough to keep me away from that hill and Nick.

Nonetheless, I didn't want to go to the carnival. I wanted, as always, to be alone with Nick. It had been nearly a year since our first kiss out in the woods. Last summer, and all of the fall, we had touched each other infrequently. I had spent every hour I was with him aching for him to kiss me again, but he had done so only a handful of times. He was always more careful and guarded since that first day when we had ended up breathless and clinging to each other.

This was the first winter we had spent together as well. Each day, as the bus dropped me off in front of the house, I would glance over my shoulder at Max, and then head off into the woods to find Nick.

After Christmas, he had begun to kiss me every day. As the weather heated up with spring, Nick's guard had dropped and on more than one occasion he had pulled away from me, chest heaving, apologizing. He left me aching, feeling as though something I desperately wanted had ended before it began.

I was sixteen that Fourth, and I am sure anyone would say that what I felt was teenage hormones. Maybe part of it was, I don't know. But every second that I wasn't with Nick, I felt lost and anxious. When I was with him, if he wasn't touching me I would feel every cell in my body wishing he would. When he did touch me, I always wanted something *more*. I knew what it was I wanted, but the memory of such pain on my sister's face as she lay below Emery the summer before scared me over and over.

And Nick never let things go too far. I was never the one to pull away from a kiss that had gotten too eager—that was him. Often, I could tell just in how long it would take him to back away from me that he didn't really want to stop either.

That morning, the heat had been intense when I left the house before seven, Max was sleeping, as he had been when I had gotten home at nearly midnight the night before. I smiled all the way through the woods, the speed of my steps increasing the closer I got. I was in a near frenzy when I had reached the opening, to find Nick standing there waiting for me.

He looked up when he heard me coming, and a broad smile covered his face. "I've been waiting," he said, stepping towards me. I reached him, and he threw both arms around my waist and pulled me to him.

"It's so early, how are you up?" I asked, but his mouth found mine before he answered. He kissed me greedily, his hands on my back pulling me closer. Then his fingers were pressing into me with a sort of desperation. Then one hand was traveling up my back and into my hair. The other hand ventured down below my waist, and then up under my shirt to rest on my back. The feeling of his skin on mine was soothing and exciting. He moved his face from mine, and onto my neck.

My breath was coming in short, desperate gasps when he finally pulled away from me. I wrapped my arms around him and laid my head on his chest before he could step too far away from me. "Good morning," I whispered. "Why are you here so early?"

"Because I wanted to see you," he said. I looked up at him and he cupped my chin in his hands. "Sorry about that, I just . . . "

His voice trailed off right as I clapped my hand over his mouth. "Please stop apologizing. You make me think you regret . . . this."

I felt his mouth twist into a smile under my hand, and he pulled me into another hug until my hand fell away. "No, I just don't want to be ungentlemanly." This was a frequent explanation. Nick didn't want me to think he wasn't a gentleman. It was ironic, to me, as he was, by far, the gentlest person I knew.

He grabbed my hand and we walked up the hill and sat down.

"Max wants us to go to the carnival in town with him tonight," I said.

"Why?" he asked, a strange tone creeping into his voice.

"I told him we were leaving last night. He was . . . mad," I said. "When he calmed down, he asked if we would go with him, since this will be our last Fourth here."

Nick smiled, and without warning, lunged towards me. He gently knocked me onto my back and leaned over me. He brushed the hair off my face, ran his finger down my nose and onto my mouth. "Our last Fourth here," he repeated. "By this time next summer, we'll be far away from here."

"No more drunks," I said.

"No more people just disappearing out of your life," he said.

"Well, unless Max comes, I will be the only person in your life. Me and Molly, at least," I pointed out.

His face grew serious. "I think I am OK with that." He kissed me again, but after a moment I shoved against him and pushed him away.

"Nice try to distract me but you haven't answered my question."

Nick rolled onto his side and faced me. "I forget what you even asked me."

I groaned in false annoyance and stared at the sky. "Come to the carnival tonight with me and Max," I said.

He paused. "OK," he said finally, and somewhat sadly.

"You don't want to," I said simply.

"You asked me to and I will," he said.

"It's for Max, Nick. I can't tell you how I feel, lately, how horrible I am for pushing him out . . . " I suddenly felt tears well in my eyes. I hadn't even known they were threatening.

"Hey, hey, hey," he said, propping up on an elbow to look at me. "Your brother is still welcome here, any time, and you know that." I nodded weakly. "And if I remember, it was him and that typewriter that led to us being here alone so much." I nodded again, thinking back fuzzily to how this had began three or four summers ago.

But, no matter what Nick said, he couldn't understand. "But Nick, us, this, I've never been without Max, you can't understand.

My whole life it has been the two of us, taking care of each other. And now I am leaving. I offered to let him come, but I didn't let him be part of the plan. I feel like I have betrayed him, and I promise you, the things he said last night when I told him let me know that he thinks that, too."

"What did he say?" he asked.

I quickly regretted mentioning it. I didn't keep things from Nick, but repeating my brother's words would make him mad, I was sure. "He said," I began, before taking a deep breath, "that you probably told me we could leave together because you would do anything to . . . "

I looked at his face, painted with concern for me and began to cry again.

"Menna, it's OK. Whatever Max said, he said because he was upset."

I clamped my hand over my eyes in a ridiculous attempt to hide the tears. Nick rested his hand on my stomach.

"I know."

"So what is it that I would do anything to do?" he asked.

I took a deep breath and rolled onto my side to face him. "Fuck me," I said simply.

"Ah," Nick said, making a clear effort to keep his face composed, though we was obviously upset. "Max thinks all I want from you is sex, then?"

"No! You just said yourself that he said it out of anger. And I told him that it wasn't that. That you had never even tried . . . that we . . . I mean, we never . . . " I couldn't find the right words, and for once was relieved to find Nick smiling at my blatant embarrassment. "He apologized within minutes. He knows that isn't it."

"Good," Nick said, and laid back. I put my head on his chest, and we rested there silently for what must have been hours.

That evening, the memory of our peaceful day began to feel far away; I was showered and changed and waiting for him to arrive. Max was downstairs. Momma was out, and Lily had left with Emery an hour before.

I had one dress, which was a hand-me-down of Lily's. It was black, with little white flowers, and tiny straps. It was shorter than I was comfortable with, and I had to put a small sweater over it to cover my bra straps. Really, it was too hot for the sweater, but I liked the way the neckline of the dress sloped down, and how the black matched my hair and the white my skin, so I decided to suffer through the sweater. I wanted to look nice, inexplicably, for the man who saw me in cut-off jeans and ragged tee-shirts every day. I had even braided my long hair carefully and neatly, and put on some make-up.

Max looked up when I walked downstairs. "You look pretty, Menn," he said, and I blushed as I thanked him. This was a rare moment, the two of us together and alone in the living room. Outside of the comfortable and familiar attic, something seemed awkward.

"Did you put the dress on for Nick?" he asked, staring blankly into the television.

"I just figured if I was going to go to this town thing, I might as well look nice," I lied.

"Is he nice to you?" Max asked.

"What kind of dumb question is that?" I demanded. "You know Nick. Of course he is."

Max met my eyes. "You're right. I'm sorry. I just want to make sure someone is taking care of you, since I don't see you much to do it myself."

"I can take care of myself, Max." I remembered the ridiculous conversation he and my mother had held at the breakfast table years before, and thought with amazement over the fact that Max obviously still believed it.

"Menna, just because you *can* take care of yourself doesn't mean you shouldn't have someone else to help," he said. "I know you *can*, but I like knowing that you have help."

"Who looks after you, Max?" I asked. Guilt over abandoning him so much these past months replaced my sudden burst of anger.

"Menna, it's always been harder to hurt me than it has you," he said.

A knock on the door ended the conversation, and I walked out of the room to answer it. Nick stood there in his best jeans with a white button-up shirt tucked into them. He looked me up and down. "You're beautiful," he said simply, and handed me a flower, kissed me on the cheek, and walked in to get Max.

We were about to leave when I touched my wrist and excused myself to dash back upstairs. The dress had no pockets, and so I had to wear the bracelet Nick had made me. I couldn't leave without it.

We had to walk through much of the town to get to the carnival, but even half a mile away, we could see the lights and hear the crowd. This was our town's biggest event of the year, and clearly everyone was out for it.

I was between Max and Nick, and Nick always seemed to be just a few inches out of reach. I wasn't able to grab his hand, and I wondered if that was because of Max or because of the town. We walked in silence, but much had passed between us all on the walk over.

The carnival was small compared to those I have seen since, but at the time, the tilt-a-whirl, ferris wheel, and small stage surrounded by scattered booths seemed to be the whole world.

"What should we do first?" I asked as we entered. Max and Nick were looking at each other in a weird way, as though they each thought themselves to be the third wheel.

Max stared at his feet. "I'm gonna play some games," he said. "Can I catch up with you two later?"

I had to quell a rising anger. He had made us come along, pulled us here, and was now acting as though he wished we hadn't come. Nonetheless, his offer made it possible for Nick and me to be alone, and I was grateful for it. I turned to Nick. "I've never been on a ferris wheel. Wanna do that?"

Nick nodded silently, and we walked off in that direction.

A crowd swelled around us and I instinctively reached for his hand. He pulled away and I turned to face him with confusion on my face. He looked concerned and uneasy. "It's not a good idea, Menn," he explained. "Let's not draw attention to ourselves."

"I don't care what these people think," I said, a little too loudly as a few turned to look at me in a quizzical way. They then looked at Nick, his long hair pulled back, and a wave of disgust passed their faces.

Nick stepped close to me and leaned in to my ear. His arms were pinned to his side as though it was taking a conscious effort not to touch me. "I care what they *do*," he whispered, and set off in the crowd ahead of me, glancing over his shoulder periodically to ensure I was still behind him.

We got in the ferris wheel line, which was short. The other ride was packed with people. The town always ran all of the rides and booths for free—most of the yearly budget went into making this event memorable and fun—but even being free, the ferris wheel was not a draw.

We only had to wait for one group to go before us, though they must have ridden for a solid five minutes. Nick stood as far away from me as he could in the line without looking like we weren't waiting together. "I hate this," I finally whispered as loud as I could, hoping only he would hear me.

"I know," he whispered back. We were always alone when we were together, and we were always so close, touching, holding hands. I felt lost with him so near and not having his arm around me.

Finally, it was our turn for the ride, and we climbed into the wide booth. If the carnie noticed the white girl and the Indian together, he didn't make it known. He closed the bar with Nick as far across the seat from me as he could get, and up we went.

Once we were above the crowd, he wordlessly pushed his hand across the cold metal seat and found mine.

"I see you're wearing your bracelet," he said, staring straight ahead. "I've never seen you wear it before."

"I always have it," I said, looking at his profile. I felt somehow defiant this far above everything. "I always have it with me. I keep it in my pocket because I am scared of losing it."

"You've carried that thing in your pocket every day for the last two years?"

"Yes," I said simply, and took a deep breath. "Will you tell me what the word means?"

His smile faded and he looked away, nodding a little. "It means *love*, Menna. It means I love you."

Though I knew I loved him, and knew he loved me, these were words we'd never said. There was something serious and intense about the way he said it now, as though the word itself were sacred. "You've loved me for the last two years?" I asked, barely able to force the words out.

He looked up and met my gaze. "I've loved you for much longer than that."

We were descending in the wheel, plummeting back towards the crowd of people. I wanted to throw my arms around him and kiss him and touch him and be near him, but I knew I couldn't. I looked ahead out towards the crowd as he gently pulled his hand away so no one on the ground would see.

"Oh," I said silently. "You know that I love you, too, right?" I said quietly.

He smiled in a small way, looking down. "I do now," he said.

"You ever doubted it?" I asked.

He turned to face me. "Menna, this place, our lives, this is terrible. I know you want to leave with me, I know you want to be away from here. And I know you care about me. But I've never been quite sure, not until right now knowing that you always have that silly thing in your pocket, that you wanted to leave with *me* and not just wanted to leave with someone."

My mouth dropped open. "Of course it's you, Nick, of course. You're . . . I need . . . I can't . . . how could . . . ?"

And he was laughing at me again.

"I love it when you're at a loss for words," he said.

But I found some, some that I meant with everything in me. "I want you to stop worrying about being ungentlemanly. I want all of you."

He wouldn't look at me. "No, you don't."

"Don't tell me what I want, Nick. I know what I want. I want you."

"So you can prove Max wrong? You want me to fuck you so you can prove that I will stick around afterwards?" he asked.

"I don't like that word," I said quietly, a little hurt by what he had said.

"I don't either," he said.

"It's not about Max, Nick," I said, now playing with my hands that were folded in my lap. "It's about you and me."

He didn't say anything, just stared off into the distance.

"You can almost see the lights of Mobile from here."

He was changing the subject. I felt instantly angry. "Maybe you're so focused on being a gentleman because you're not interested in doing anything more than kissing me," I whispered, more to myself than anything.

"God, Menna, sometimes you can be kind of stupid," he said suddenly, rather loudly, with anger in his voice.

I was too shocked to reply, and he turned to look directly at me. We were again at the top of the wheel, and it lurched to a stop as the carnie began unloading passengers beneath us. The ride was soon to come to an end. Nick continued, a hurry in his voice.

"I want everything you want. God, trust me, I want it so badly that . . . but you're young and you're hurt by everything here. I can't take advantage of that, not until we're out of here, away from this place and you know for sure that what you want now is always what you will want," he said. Three cars remained in front of us to be unloaded.

"Nick, none of this hurts when I'm with you," I said. "None of it. None of it matters. God, between you and Max and everyone feeling like I need to be protected all the time . . . I don't. I'm not that young, you know. And I am tired of being told that I don't know my own mind."

He looked at me and nodded as the ride came to an end and we climbed off.

Chapter Seven

Max shakes off sleep quickly and grabs the ringing phone. "What?" he demands of the receiver.

"Wake up call, Mr. Soother," the operator says.

Max smiles despite himself, hearing not the expected sterile motel-front-desk voice, but instead a thick Southern accent. "Thanks," he mumbles, and hangs up the phone.

The room, like the operator's voice, screams of the South. The painting on the wall shows a cowboy wrestling a steer. He shakes his head, mutters "Texas" to himself, then searches for a room service menu. There isn't one, so he showers quickly and sets out in search of someplace to eat.

He finds a small diner and settles into a sticky booth. The waitress comes over and slides into the seat across from him. She is young, probably twenty, and has a lightness about her. Her brown curly hair is pulled up into a tight ponytail, but even the stark hairstyle can't detract from the softness of her pale face. She smiles at him, her huge brown eyes alight. "Can I take your order?"

He instinctively glances around the place, and notices that he's the only one there. "Bored?" he asks.

As though this question signifies genuine interest in her state, she sighs and flops her head dramatically down onto the table. "You have no idea. I can't wait to get outta here."

"Got a long day ahead of you?" he asks.

"Long months ahead of me," she says, sitting up and resting her head on her hands. "I'm leaving for college the end of August and I just can't wait."

The more he looks at her the more he sees the desire to talk about herself brimming over. It oozes from every pore, from her big brown eyes. He smiles at her, remembering being eighteen and knowing he would have been just as excited for a chance to go to college.

"Where you going?" he asks.

"Princeton," she says.

He raises his eyebrows. "Princeton?"

"What? You don't think a little thing from all the way down here can get into a big ole school like Princeton?" she teases. "I got in no problem, now I just gotta fatten up my bank account so I don't starve while I'm there." She winks at him and picks up her pad and paper.

"What are you going to study at Princeton?" he asks.

"Biology," she says. "I'm going to be a doctor."

"What kind of doctor?"

"I don't know that yet, I just know a doctor," she says.

He nods and looks at the menu while she taps her pen and her feet anxiously. Her whole body emanates excitement, and Max decides he genuinely likes this girl. "Can I have a cup of coffee and some pancakes?" he asks.

"Coming right up," she grins, jumping up without writing his order, and heading off.

Max stares out the window and begins to think over his plan for the day, but has barely gotten beyond getting on the highway when the waitress returns with two cups of coffee. She sits down across from him and hands him one, while sipping the other one herself. "I hope you don't mind, but I am just dying to talk to an unfamiliar face, and you look awful lonely."

"I don't mind," Max says, sipping his coffee black. He sets the cup down and tugs at the corner of his lip.

"So what do you do?" she asks.

"I'm a writer," he says.

"Like John Grisham?" she asks, her eyes growing wide. Max wonders if they will soon cover her entire face.

"More like Dear Abbey."

She stares back at him blankly before deciding to change the subject. "Where you heading?" she says. "I know you're not from around here. You definitely ain't Texan."

"Better watch words like 'ain't' at Princeton," he says. "They chew you up and spit you out up North if they hear a twang."

"Oh, I know," she says. "I think it's just sick the kind of judgments people make about other people over stupid things like accents."

"Yes, it is," he agrees, and sips his coffee. "And I am headed towards a small town just west of Mobile."

"*West* of Mobile? What the heck you want down there? It's nothing but heat, humidity, and Indians."

He stares at her sharply and she shrinks back into the seat. "I'm sorry," she says reflexively, "I'm sure it's a real nice place."

"It's hell," he says, though his face softens, "but it's home."

"Oh, you're going home," she says, smiling again as though his silent admonition had gone unnoticed. "Where you coming from?"

"A reservation out west," he says.

"An Indian reservation?" she asks. Color creeps into her cheeks and he smiles inwardly at her embarrassment.

"Yes."

"You don't look like no Indian," she says.

"And you don't look like a Princeton student," he replies.

She regards him for a minute as though trying to decide if he is joking or not, then laughs it off.

"Speaking of which, why Princeton?"

She smiles broadly. "Ain't no Ivy League in the South."

"No, there sure isn't," he says.

She chats with him all through his breakfast, and even finishes the last of his pancakes. He begins to understand why his questions always annoyed Menna so much.

As he leaves and gets out on the road, he tries to remember if he ever understood Menna.

Max

I watched my sister and Nick the whole time they were on that ride, watched them go up and down, their mouths moving. They didn't touch each other, from what I could see, but I noticed a few people around me looking at them, too. They definitely stood out—well, Nick at least, who was not only the only Indian at the fair, but was massively tall, especially compared to Menna—but it wasn't even the way they looked.

The way they were with each other, even here among all of these people, couldn't be hidden simply by not touching. They moved almost in sync, even when they weren't looking at each other. The space between them was tense, as though it was simply wrong to have that space at all.

As they got out of the car, Menna tripped, and Nick reached for her arm without hesitation. The carnie got to her first, and stared long and hard at Nick as Menna stepped down.

From behind me, I heard Emery and Jimmy Reid. There were others with them, adding the periodic affirmation or restating what Emery and Jimmy said, but their two voices carried on the conversation that convinced me that Nick and Menna should not be here. Asking them to come had been a mistake.

I had wanted them here, wanted the three of us to be together so badly on a place that wasn't the hill, wasn't theirs, I hadn't thought enough about it. This was the town, and the town belonged to everyone but us, and especially everyone but Nick. This had been selfish and stupid, and Nick had known it, and Menna probably had, too, but they did it for me.

"Your girlfriend's sister sure does have a thing for the redskins," Jimmy said. "Does that run in the family?"

"Fuck you, Jimmy," Emery said. "Lily ain't like that little bitch at all."

"That little bitch should know better," Jimmy added. "What does he think he's doing over here?"

"Maybe we should go remind him where the fence is," Emery added. There was a deep menace in his voice that filled me with fear. I walked off as quickly as I could through the crowd to find Nick and Menna, suddenly grateful for Nick's height. The top of his head always appeared above the sea of people.

I caught up with them and glanced over my shoulder. Emery and Jimmy hadn't moved from where they were, but were staring straight at me with interest, as if they realized I must have heard it all.

"Max," Menna said, forcing a smile, but the weight of whatever conversation she had been having with Nick clearly still on her mind. Her face was confused and pensive. "What do you want to do now?" she asked.

"We need to go," I said urgently.

"We just got here," she said.

I glanced over my shoulder again to see Emery and Jimmy moving through the crowd towards us. Nick followed my gaze and saw them. His expression didn't change, as he suddenly said, "We have to go, now."

"We can lose them in the crowd," I said, "but Nick, you have to stoop down so they can't see your head."

"I'm not hiding," he said to me. "I just want to get Menna out of here so she doesn't get pulled in to anything."

He grabbed me by the arm, and looked towards Menna so I knew I was to take her hand, and he pulled us both through the crowd away from Emery and Jimmy. He moved quickly and gracefully. I bumped and thudded into more people than he did, apologizing while I went and holding on to Menna with a tight grip. From the look on her face, she clearly resented our quickly whisking her away without asking her what she thought. However, she also knew what would happen if Emery and Jimmy caught up with us and wanted to avoid a confrontation.

When we cleared the parking lot and were walking back into town, the panic I had suddenly felt cleared a bit. Nick released my arm, and I let go of Menna, who began to lag back a bit. Her face was confused and conflicted, and I could almost feel her angst.

"I think I over-reacted," I said. "I heard Emery and Jimmy talking, but maybe it was just talk."

"Jimmy will back down if it's an even fight, but Emery isn't just talk," Menna said from behind me. I turned to face her, and Nick, a few feet up, turned to look at us both. She looked up as though surprised by my reaction. "You've seen Lily's black eyes and bruised wrists, Max."

"Yeah, but it had to be Momma, the way Momma is always hitting her," I stammered.

"When's the last time you saw Momma hit Lily?" she asked, and I thought back. Actually, it was the day Nick had carried her from her bedroom. But the bruises appeared over and over, even as my mother retreated further and further into her bottle and became more and more docile.

"He hits Lily, Max, he is violent, trust me," Nick added, and I stood between them.

Lily was a bitch, no doubt, but she was my sister. She was, perhaps, the one who always made sure dinner was available to Menna and me. She was the one who called us vagrants and refused to be seen with us. She was the reason cupcakes appeared on the table on our birthday, and now, since she was working as a cashier, the reason the house had electricity.

She was my sister and Emery had hurt her. I should have protected them both, Menna and Lily. I should have been the man of the house, but I had done nothing, casually ignoring as Menna slipped away from me and Lily was pulled away and beaten.

An intense shame and anger filled me. I looked from Menna to Nick and back to Menna, with no idea what to say or what to do.

I felt my hands ball into fists, but in truth, the only person I wanted to hurt was myself. Nothing, I had done nothing while both of my sisters slipped away from me. I had left my drunk, crying mother on the attic floor, never once confronted her about the drinking that had destroyed our family.

I had done nothing, nothing, except bring Menna, who was sweet and kind despite her angry pride, into a situation where she could get hurt. I wasn't a man. I was less than a boy. I had done nothing.

Nick seemed to sense what was going on in me, because he stepped close to me and put his hand on my shoulder. "Max, this isn't your fault," he said. "Menna is safe, I promise you. Lily made her choices. But look at that man," he said, nodding towards the end of the street. Emery, Jimmy, and two of their friends were moving quickly towards us. Emery was easily six inches taller than I was, though still not quite as massive as Nick, with arms the size of my legs. I stared down at my own body, skinny and pale. I could type faster than anyone at school, but look at me now. What good was I going to be in this situation? I wasn't a man.

Nick continued. "All we can do now is get Menna out of here. The two of us can't do much against the four of them," he said, and we both looked at Menna, who stood off to the side silently. She looked scared. The street was deserted, it was just us.

I looked to Menna and simply said, "Go." She nodded and the three of us began walking quickly away from the approaching group. They were maybe two hundred yards behind us. Their silence as they approached was disconcerting. I reach for Menna's hand, and she took mine, and we all wordlessly began walking faster.

The fireworks at the carnival began behind us, a ringing sequence of "pop, pop, pop." The shadows fell on the pavement, and the sound masked the sound of feet running towards us. Menna was suddenly wrenched away from me. Nick and I both turned to find Emery and Jimmy facing us. Their friends were gone, but Emery had Menna tightly around the waist, held to him.

"Faggots," he said in greeting, as kindly as he might have said, "Good evening" to his grandmother.

"Hello, Emery," Nick said coolly, "Jimmy."

"What do you think you're doing out here, redskin?" Jimmy shot at him.

"I was at the carnival with my friends, and we would like to leave, now, if you could let Menna go," Nick said with shocking civility. His fists were clenching and unclenching, and I knew he was angry.

"Oh see, that's the problem," Emery said. He turned to look at Menna, grabbed her chin with his other hand and examined her closely. "We know you was there, we just don't know why you thought it was OK to be there."

"My mistake, Emery," Nick said. "It won't happen again. Let her go and we'll be on our way."

I caught Menna's eye and could tell that, beneath the fear, she was livid. Any moment she was going to spout off at the mouth or go for Emery and make the situation worse. I shook my head slightly at her. She bristled, and looked back to Nick.

"Should we let 'em go, Jimmy?" Emery asked, not taking his eyes from Nick. "Or should we remind this prairie nigger what happens when you venture outside of the fence?"

"I think we should remind him," Jimmy said.

Emery nodded, and then turned his attention towards Menna. "Is she sweet, Nick, this one? Does it make you hot to fuck a white woman?" Emery ran his fingers up and down Menna's face.

"I'm not fucking any white women, Emery," Nick said calmly, but his stance betrayed that he was about to lose his calm. I noticed Menna look towards him. "Let her go, and you can teach me all of the lessons you want."

"So you're not doing it for him, eh, sweetheart?" Emery said to Menna. "You're not much like your sister, then. She'll spread her legs for anyone."

"Even you," Menna said with disdain through clenched teach. Emery grabbed her chin roughly and looked at her for a long

116

moment. Then he pushed her towards us slightly. She was facing them, halfway between us, and just about to back up when Emery swung at her. He punched her clean in the left eye, sending her reeling backwards to the ground.

Nick was on him faster than I thought possible, knocking him to the ground. He hit him once, twice, before I turned to pick Menna up off the ground. Her nose was bleeding and her eye was swelling already.

Jimmy ran to where Nick had Emery pinned and kicked Nick in the ribs. Nick rolled off of Emery and onto his back. Jimmy came over and kicked him in the face as Emery struggled to get up. Nick was to his knees and almost back on his feet when we heard a voice calling from down the street. "What's going on down there?"

We looked up to see four or five people wandering up the street, retreating home as the fireworks ended. One of them was the mayor, Jimmy's father.

Jimmy looked at him and darted off onto a side street. Emery wasn't far behind him. We got Nick to his feet and began walking home before any of the people reached us.

We crossed most of the distance in silence. As soon as we were on Thorton Street and far enough away that no one would see, Nick put his arm around Menna and pulled her to him. He couldn't look at her, I noticed, with the blood crusting on her lip. Already her eye looked bad, black and blue and nearly swollen shut. Nick had taken Jimmy's kick to the forehead and there was a gash above his right eye. It bled a little, but mostly just looked red and angry. I couldn't imagine how his ribs must feel. And here I was, unscathed, the only one of us who hadn't been hurt. I wasn't a man.

We were about to reach the house when I turned to face them. "I'm sorry," I said. "I am so sorry."

Nick waved his hand. "It's not your fault, Max."

I looked at Menna, at her one open eye. "I let him hit you. I let him hit both of you." I didn't know if I meant Nick and Menna, or Menna and Lily.

Nick dropped his arm from around her and stepped away. "Neither one of us did a very good job of keeping them from hurting her," he said, and walked briskly past us and into the woods.

Menna watched him go, clearly wanting to follow. She kept looking to me, seeing the anguish on my face. I wasn't a man, and now she was too worried about me to go with the one who had fought for her.

"Max," she said quietly, "one more year and we are all out of here. You're going to come with us. We'll be a family, finally, and this will all be over. By next June, we're gone."

The lights were on in the house. The street grew quiet enough for us to hear the bottle drop, and my mother curse.

"Go with Nick," I told her. "I'll take care of this." I turned and went into the house, as she wordlessly took off into the woods.

Menna

I could hear Nick walking ahead of me, and I knew he could hear me behind him, but he didn't stop or move back towards me. I let him go, but continued to follow. My eye hurt like hell but more than that I was desperate to calm him down.

Finally, as we neared the clearing and the hill, I called for him to stop, and he did. But he didn't turn to look at me. I walked up behind him and put my arms around him. He flinched as I touched his ribs. Then he didn't move at all, but stood there silently, his chest heaving, as I leaned on him.

"Please," I said into his shirt. I don't know what I was pleading with him about but it was all I could think to say.

He still didn't move, but I began to feel him quaking softly. "Does it hurt?" he asked.

"I've been hit harder," I said.

He stepped away from me. "I didn't stop it," he said, finally turning to look at me. He put his hand under my chin and looked hard at my eye and nose. "I let him hit you."

"You were trying to keep it from turning into a fight."

"I did an excellent job," he said, and turned away from me again, shaking in anger.

"Nick, please," I said. "I know you're upset, but you're hurt. I'm hurt. A lot has happened. I need you, I need for you to calm down. Please."

His face changed, and he stepped towards me and pulled me next to him. "I'm sorry, Menn, you're right." He held me for a long time in the silence, his face in my hair. I clung to him, feeling safe.

We heard a rumbling of thunder in the distance. "You should go home," he said. "It's going to rain."

"I don't want to go," I said, the thought of walking away scared the hell out of me. "Let's go somewhere we won't get wet."

"Like where?" he said.

"The cottage you showed me—do Lily and Emery still go there?" I asked.

"I haven't seen them there since that day," he said. "In fact, that was the only time I ever saw them there."

"Do you go there often?" I asked.

"I sleep there, upstairs, most nights," he said. "At least for the last two or three months."

"Take me there," I said.

He looked at me with a skeptical look. "Why?" he asked.

I stared back at him, equally skeptical. "I need to be with you right now. I can't go home, yet."

He nodded, took my hand, and led me into the woods. We walked for a long time, long after the rain had started and slowly drenched us both. We finally reached the ramshackle house that I had seen only once before. It looked even more rundown than I remembered.

"I thought you weren't able to get in here," I said.

"I found a way," he said, and reached down and popped a screen out of place near the ground. He beckoned for me to climb down into the house, and I did. My dress pulled up around my waist as I did, and I was glad that I went in first, so I could smooth it out before Nick saw me.

He came in behind me, and pointed to some rickety stairs at the far end of the room. We climbed up them to the upstairs, to a small room. There was a rug on the floor, with a few pillows and a

119

blanket pushed off the side. It smelled like mold, and water was dripping from the roof into a puddle in a far corner.

"It's kind of gross in here," he said apologetically, and began moving things around. "But I have some water over here," he walked across the room and fetched a bottle from against the wall, and picked up a towel. "Sit down?"

I sat cross-legged in the middle of the carpet. It was thick and soft, though a bit dingy, on the back of my legs. Nick sat across from me, pouring water onto the towel and wiping the blood from around my nose. He cleaned it up quickly and quietly, and then put the washcloth aside and stared past me at the wall.

"Nick, please talk to me," I said finally.

He looked at my face, and then said suddenly, "Let's go tonight."

"What?" I asked.

"Look, I've been saving every cent I could get, I have a little bit of money, let's just go."

"We can't, Nick," I said.

"Why?" he asked, looking at me with desperation in his eyes. "Your mother wouldn't even notice if you were gone."

"Yeah, but I have one more year of school, and the school would look for me if I didn't show up. They would go to my mom; they would look for us. I don't want to hide for a year, and I don't want you to get in trouble for running away with an underage girl. We can do this, we can do this for eleven more months," I said.

He shook his head and looked away. "I just . . . I can't . . . " he stammered.

I smiled. "It's not often that you are speechless."

He turned to look at me, his face dark and serious. "God, Menna, if anything happened to you . . . "

"Nothing is going to happen to me, I promise. It's you and me, from here on out," I said, touching his face.

He looked at me and suddenly moved quickly to me. I was flat on my back with him on top of me in a moment, and he was kissing me desperately. I kissed him back, trying to keep up with him but barely being able to breathe. He kissed my mouth, my cheeks, my neck, viciously, almost angrily.

I put my hands on his chest, wrapped them around his neck. He mouth was at the base of my throat and then moving down to my chest. I grabbed a fistful of his shirt and sighed more loudly than I intended to. His hand ran down my side, to my leg, pulled my knee up. I wrapped it around his waist and pulled at the neckline of his shirt trying to pull his head back up to mine. I wanted him, wanted this, but not out of desperation or anger.

His hand ran up my leg under my skirt, his head moving further down my chest reaching the low neckline of my dress. He moved back up my neck when I said his name quietly.

His head shot up, and he pushed his arms straight so he was hovering above me. "I am sorry, I am so sorry." He rolled to his side, laying beside me and staring at the ceiling.

"I asked you to stop apologizing," I said, smiling. I rolled onto my side, put my hand on the waist of his jeans, ran it up under his shirt and onto his chest. I leaned over and kissed his neck. He put his hand over my hand, and I thought he was going to stop me, but instead he rolled towards me until our mouths met, and he kissed me softly for a very long time. He finally broke away and looked hard at me.

"Menna, I love you so much," he said.

"I love you, too," I said, and he kissed me again. I reached down and pulled at the hem of his shirt, pulling it up over his head. He ran his hands up my legs, under my dress, and then quickly reached around me to unzip it. I shrugged out of my sweater to help him, looking for a moment at him, next to me, his shirt off. I had never seen his chest before, and he looked so still.

We jointly pushed my dress down, off my shoulders until my bra was exposed, and then further down. Nick kissed me again, and, with my eyes closed, I felt him struggling slightly to pull his jeans off without breaking away from me.

He unhooked my bra, kissed my breasts in a soft, passing way as I pushed my underwear off. I was naked on the rug.

I had a moment of panic, not knowing what came next or what to do. I pulled apart from him. "Have you done this before?" I asked.

"Just once," he said. "Are you scared?"

"I don't know what to do," I said, looking away.

"We don't have to do this now," he said, carefully touching my bruised eye. "We have all the time in the world, this can wait."

"No, I don't want to wait," I said.

Nick smiled, kissed my nose once, my lips once, the purple forming around my eye. His hand traveled down my stomach, over my hips, to where my legs met. I hadn't realized I had them clamped together until he gently pushed them apart and rolled fully onto me.

"I love you," he whispered again, and then I felt a sharp and sudden pain. I inhaled.

"I'm sorry," he said, and began to move like he was going to stop. I threw my arm around his waist and held him to me.

"Don't," I said, and arched my back so our faces met and kissed him. He kissed me back and rocked into me, and in a moment the pain subsided. Then it was just us, me and him, together.

After a while, I found myself lying next to him. He was behind me, his chest pressed into my back, arm slung around my hip, running his lips lazily along my neck and shoulders.

"Who was it?" I asked finally.

"Who was what?" he asked.

"The one other time?" I asked.

"You really want to talk about that now?" he asked, pulling his mouth away from my skin and talking into my hair.

"We don't have to talk about it, I just want to know."

"It was a girl visiting my cousin, when I was fourteen," he said.

"Oh," I said softly.

"Does that bother you?"

"No," I said.

"Are you sure?" he asked.

I twisted to look at him. "I'm sure," I said. "I'm happy now, I just wanted to know."

"Did I hurt you?" he asked.

"For a second, but then . . . " I said, smiling in a soft, embarrassed way.

"Then . . . " he smiled, and kissed me again. "Should I walk you home? I don't want Max to worry."

"He knows I'm with you," I said. "I don't want to leave, I want to wake up here tomorrow with you."

We had the blanket lazily tossed over us. It was dirty and itchy, and barely big enough for one, much less two. Though the day had been hot, the rain had cooled the night down considerably. The room was dark, and chilly, and I could hear things scurrying around downstairs, but none of it mattered. I had never felt a peace like I felt at that moment.

"How does your head feel?" I asked. I had been careful to avoid this subject since we'd arrived, but everything seemed calmer now, and that run-in with Emery and Jimmy was a distant memory.

"It hurts. How's your eye?"

"It hurts."

He made a weird noise, somewhere between a snort and an angry grunt. "I swear to God, Menna, you and your mouth." He chuckled to himself as he rolled onto his back. I felt his warmth move away from me and it filled me with a momentary panic, until he reached up and pulled me down to him.

"You're blaming this on me?" I said elbowing him, but smiling.

"No, I am blaming it on them, but . . . they may have been happy just beating on me if you hadn't had to open your mouth," he threw his right arm up over his eyes. The words were chiding, but his voice smiled as he said it. His left arm was around me, tracing circles on my stomach.

"Well, I am sorry if my mouth offends you," I said, fake pouting.

"It's actually one of the things I love most about you. Your temper is a bit much at times, but I love that you are passionate enough to get that angry. So I even love it when you're mad over nothing," he said.

I settled into him. "So this friend of your cousin's . . . "

Nick groaned and stood up. It was dark in the room, but I

watched him hunt around for his pants, which were balled up near the wall. I gathered the blanket around me. I'd never seen him, or any other man, fully naked before, and I was content to watch him move. He didn't seem to notice or mind. He finally found them and pulled them on in one swift motion.

"I guess me and my mouth are annoying you again," I said, starting to look around for my dress.

"No," he said. "And I get that this matters to you, and I know there are a lot of reasons why it would, so just tell me which one is the why." He sat down facing me without reaching for his shirt, for which I was grateful. "Do you think somehow being with you is less important to me because I was with someone else first?"

"No, well, not until you just said it, I didn't," I said, looking down. I was being silly, and I knew I was being silly, but something about it just wouldn't leave my head.

"Menna, I got kicked in the face and the ribs, called all sorts of names, watched you get hurt, got rained on, and despite all that, I can tell you without hesitation that this was the best night of my life," he said, leaning onto one elbow and tracing his fingers up and down the front of my leg.

"Mine, too," I said. "I didn't know, I mean I guess, I knew that this would be amazing, but just this, now, here with you, everything feels OK. I don't want to leave this room."

"Then what, what is it?"

"You're mad," I said, and lay onto my back.

"No, I'm not, I just want to know what about this bothers you so I can try to fix it," he said. I couldn't see him, but I felt his lips around my navel, slowly moving their way up my stomach.

He had made it to the bottom of my rib cage. "You're making it hard to concentrate so we can talk about this," I sighed.

He pulled away, and there was suddenly cold for a moment. Then Nick lay down beside me, and I turned my head to look at him.

"Menna, talk to me," he said.

"I think I would rather you keep doing what you were doing," I said, smiling.

"I will, once you tell me," he said, his finger touching my face.

"Were you the only other person she had been with?" I asked.

"No," he said simply.

"Were you together more than once?' I asked.

"No," he said.

"Was she . . . " I took a breath and looked directly at him, "good, you know, at it?"

Unexpectedly, Nick laughed out loud. "Is *that* what you are worried about?"

My pride was hurt, and I quickly rolled away from him and again hunted for my dress. "Menna, Menna," he said behind me. His hands were on my shoulders, circling gently, and his mouth right at my ear.

"I'm worried because you didn't tell me until now, and I am worried because I don't know what I am doing, and I am just scared that you will be thinking about her and comparing us," the words tumbled out of me. I felt him begin to kiss my neck, his left arm circling my waist and pulling me close to him.

"I didn't tell you until now because I didn't want you to worry about her, but when you asked me, I wasn't going to lie," he mumbled. "And trust me, once before doesn't make me an expert. I think we're supposed to learn this stuff together." His hand found my breast, his mouth still on my neck and my ear. "And I promise you, when I am with you, and when I am not with you, you are the *only* thing on my mind."

Before I knew it I was under him on the floor again, trying to hold myself as close to him as I possibly could. After a moment, he moved a few inches from me and smiled sadly. "You know what's funny?"

"What," I asked.

"We just had a normal argument," he said. I thought for a moment and he was right. I was sure that many other guys had talked to their sixteen-year-old girlfriends and told them not to worry about the time he was with someone else.

"I guess so," I said, "but why is that funny?"

"We don't normally talk about anything, well, *normal*," he said, and then he kissed me again, and I fumbled for the button on his pants, and we forgot about everyone else until well after dawn the next morning.

Chapter Eight

*M*enna pulls off the highway, and her stomach begins to sink. She still recognizes that small church off to the right, and the sign out front is still warning her that Jesus is coming soon. Jesus, it seemed, had been on His way since she left. Beyond that, there are a lot of new buildings, new construction she wasn't expecting.

"Are we here?" Cole asks expectantly.

"Yes," Menna says quietly.

"You don't sound too happy."

Menna forces a smile. "Cole, I left this place because I hated it, and now I am back here."

Cole looks away thoughtfully. "So why did it have to be here? Why didn't you have Max come to Albany?"

Menna nods to herself. "Well, you told me it was time I finally told you about your family, and I think you deserve to know, and this place is so much a part of that family. It had to be here."

"When do we get into town?" Cole asks, staring at one lone fast food restaurant.

Menna chuckles and turns onto Maple. "Honey, this *is* town."

Cole's head shoots around. "What?"

"Hey, there's more here now then when I lived here. They at least have a motel now, sort of."

"We can't stay with my grandmother?" Cole asks.

"No," Menna says, more defensively than she intended to. Cole looks at her, bewildered. "Honey, I don't even know if she is still alive."

Cole's face grows dark. "How can you not know?"

"Because I haven't seen or talked to anyone here since I left, honey, seven months before you were born."

"Except my mother," Cole adds, her voice quiet and full of hurt.

"Yes, except your mother," Menna says. "Listen, Cole, my mother was not a very good person. Even if she is still alive, and even if she still lives where we did when we were kids, I don't want you to be around her much."

"But, she's my grandmother," Cole protests.

"I know," Menna says. "And we will see if we can find her. But first, I want to find the motel, and a bed. I am sick of driving, and I smell terrible, and I want to see if Max has checked in yet."

"He may be here already?" Cole asks hopefully.

"Probably not—he had a lot farther to come than we did," Menna says, "But you never know with Max."

The motel turns out to be four rooms for rent over the old deli, which was now a restaurant. She and Cole settle in quickly, after learning that Max wasn't there yet, and both fall soundly asleep.

Max

The first time Menna didn't come home for the night I didn't sleep much at all. Normally her soft snoring was my backdrop as I fought consciousness, and the silence in the attic without her was distracting. It wasn't a total surprise, as she had been coming in later and later over the past few weeks, and leaving earlier and earlier. But that night, she never wandered in.

When I had come inside, every light had been on in the house and my mother was sitting up on the couch, looking surprisingly alert. "Where you been?" she asked.

"At the carnival," I said.

"What carnival?"

"It's the Fourth of July. Didn't you hear the fireworks?"

"Yeah, I did," she said finally. I didn't see any bottles around, but she had definitely been drinking. She was in the dangerous space between docilely drunk and sober. This was the space where she might, at any moment, turn violent.

"Where's your sisters?"

"Dunno," I said, and headed for the stairs.

"Don't walk away from me when I'm talking to you," she said, and I froze.

She stood, as though to loom over me, though I was inches taller than she and she wobbled once free from the couch. I never really thought about it till then, but when she was standing my mother was a very small and frail woman.

"You three run wild like you own this place. You and Menna, always outside and romping, just like your father, fucking half-breed that he was," she spat.

"Half-breed?" I asked, but she turned from me, apparently finished with the conversation, and slumped back onto the couch. "Mom, what did you mean by that?"

She sat down angrily looking up at me like she was doing something she detested by speaking. "You're a lot like him, Max. Quiet, always thinking. Menna, I don't know. I guess she is more like me."

"What was his name?" I asked.

She opened her mouth to speak, then closed it again. Then, finally she said, "It don't matter. He run out on us, couldn't take care of anyone. I expect you'll be off, outta here before long, too."

"I'm not going anywhere, Momma," I said, almost to myself.

She pulled her knees up to her chest, rocking back and forth slightly. "I know it ain't supposed to be like this, Max."

"Like what?"

She looked at me for a long time again. I had the faint instinct to call her a drunk, to provoke her, make her hit me so I could hurt like Menna and Lily had hurt. But instead, I stood rooted. Less than a man, and, apparently, just like my father.

"Never mind," she said, getting up quickly and shakily. "I'm going out. If your sisters come home, you tell them I said they can't run wild." She stormed out the door, keys in hand. I heard her car pull away, and was left alone in the house.

I went upstairs to the attic, looked at the tattered blankets spread around, my sister's clothes strewn about with mine neatly folded in a pile under the window. We really were different, for all the similarities we had. I laid down, waiting, wishing for her to walk in. I wanted to tell her what Momma had said, wanted to finally share with her what I hoped to do next summer after I grad-uated. I wanted to apologize for being less than a man, for standing by while Emery hit her, for ever questioning what she had with Nick.

I was going over it in my head time after time while I waited for the door to open and her bare feet to pad in across the floor. The sun was nearly up when I finally fell asleep, my head awash with unspoken intimations.

I didn't sleep for very long, perhaps three or four hours, before my eyes flew open to confirm that Menna was still not there.

I dressed quickly and walked downstairs. My mother was asleep on the couch. Glancing in Lily's room, I found her in bed sleeping as well. I stepped in to look at her more closely.

She was on her back, her red hair curled around her. I looked closely at her face, at a small yellowing area below her eye. Was that a healing bruise? She had kicked the blankets off in the night, and I could see most of her arms and legs. I looked her up and down, hunting for some sign. I didn't see anything noticeable, but when my eyes returned to her face, I realized she was awake and looking at me.

"What are you doing, Max?" she asked, with uncharacteristic gentleness in her voice.

"I was looking to see if he'd hit you recently," I said.

She sat up slowly. "Who?"

"Emery. He hits you, doesn't he?"

"Shut the fuck up, Max," she said, but she sounded more scared than angry. "Get out of here."

I nodded silently, and walked towards the door. I had reached for the knob when her voice stopped me. "Max," she said gently. "I heard about what happened last night."

I turned to look at her, not sure what to say in response. She stared at me for a long moment before speaking again. "You need to stay out of town and away from Jimmy and Emery. And keep Menna and Nick away from them, too."

I nodded, wanting to tell her that I should not be trusted with taking care of Menna, wanting to tell her I would make it right for all the times Emery hit her and me, her brother, I had done nothing. But I nodded again and left silently.

As I got to the porch, I realized that I had no idea where to go. Kay was gone, and the library held no appeal for me that day. I wanted to see my sister, be near her, so desperately. I thought of the hill, thought of the strange, outcast feeling that I had had there lately. But it didn't matter. I had a clue from my mother as to where we came from, and a warning from Lily and so many words of my own that I needed to share with her. I had to go. I had to see her.

I found my way through the woods more easily this time, reaching the clearing to find them, in fact, there. I barely paused to notice that they sat, Menna in front of Nick, his arms around her, and never wondered if perhaps I would be interrupting.

Menna saw me as soon as I hit the bottom of the hill, noticed my panicked expression, and stood to greet me. Nick followed, putting his hand on her shoulder as he stood.

"Max," she said, forcing her voice to be calm, but I could tell she was concerned.

"You didn't come home," I said. I had to stop and catch my breath from running.

"I know," she said, glancing softly behind her at Nick in a knowing way. She didn't intend for me to see it, or the way his fingers tightened slightly on her shoulder. At that second I knew what they had done in the hours since I had seen them. Nick, usually so confident, so composed, met my eyes briefly and then looked away.

I stood up straight and looked at Menna for a long moment. "Max," she said, "Nick and I fell asleep, and . . . " she began to stammer.

I waived my hand to stop her from talking. "Lily said to stay away from Emery."

"Of course," Nick said.

"No, out of town, away from Emery and Jimmy until, well, you leave," I said, and turned on my heel to head down the hill.

"We leave," she called after me, and ran down the hill to grab my arm. "Max, *we* are leaving. You are coming with us."

I turned to look at her. "Maybe, Menn," I said.

She dropped my arm. "Max, you have to come, you have to."

"What about Momma and Lily, if I leave with you?"

She recoiled as though she'd been slapped. "What about them? Would they even notice if you were gone?"

I looked at the ground, then back at her. "I'll see you later, Menn," I said.

She nodded quietly, and I walked back through the woods, taking care not to look back over my shoulder. I heard her crying softly until the trees enveloped me.

I was, again, lying on the floor in the attic when she came home that night, well after dark. She tried to slip in, wondering, I suppose, if I was awake. I waited until she was also curled up on the floor before speaking.

"You OK?" I asked.

"Yeah," she said, as though the question surprised her.

"Your eye?"

She laughed softly. "Well *that* hurts. How about you?"

"I'm fine," I said.

A long, quiet moment passed while I rolled words around in my head. Questions, thoughts, statement, everything. Finally, I could only blurt out one silly-sounding question. "What's it like?"

"What?"

"Being with Nick," I said.

"You know him, you know what it's like to be around Nick." Her voice was cautious.

"Menna, I don't mean being around him. You know what I mean," I said.

"How did you know?"

"I don't know, I could just tell by the way you acted this morning," I said.

"Why are you asking me this?"

"I just, I don't know, I just want to know. You guys are so . . . easy . . . with each other," I said.

She sighed, finally saying "It was so wonderful, Max. I mean, I love him, and he loves me, and last night . . . just . . . being so close . . . I can't wait. I can't wait for the three of us to leave next year. Right after our birthday, we'll go. Nick has some money saved, and I am going to get a job this year and save some more and we will just go."

I didn't say anything. I had never heard this tone in Menna's voice before. With everything that had happened, everything in our lives, and she sounded so overwhelmingly happy. At that moment, I felt an intense desire to have what she had. It wasn't exactly like jealousy; it was more like wanting so badly to catch up when I had left so far behind.

I rolled over, away from her as her words faded and finally fell asleep.

Menna

July sixth. How much had happened in the past two days? I felt like it had been weeks since I had been in the grass with Nick and asked him to come the carnival. The strange, sometimes terrible, but mostly wonderful, progression of events had my head reeling. I began the day on the most ordinary of tasks—I was going to find a job.

I dressed in my best clothes, very aware that it was already nearly ten. Nick was going to wait for me at the hill and I wanted to finish this chore as quickly as possible so I could meet him.

Up Thorton Street and onto Maple, I searched, and hunted for any sign in a window seeking help. The town was small, but I remembered seeing these signs throughout the years up and down Maple.

I came to the deli, a small, but always busy store on the corner nearest my house, and sure enough, a sign asking for help in the window. I quickly ducked in.

Mrs. Mowry, the owner's wife, stood behind the counter. Mr. Mowry was a quiet man. When I was younger, on the very rare occasion that I was in the deli, he would wait on me with a smile, and never look twice at my grubby clothes. His wife was more observant.

"Good morning, Mrs. Mowry," I said as I approached the counter. The store was deserted, which was odd for this time of day.

"Menna," she said curtly, forcing a brief smile. "What can I do for you today?"

"I was wondering, Ma'am, if you were still looking for some help?" I said. I didn't know why I was suddenly nervous, but my hands had begun to shake.

"Help? As in a job?" she asked, her eyebrows raised. I thought they might crawl off her head.

"Yes, Ma'am. I would like a job."

She stared me straight in the eye for a full minute, as though she thought it were a prank. And then she sighed heavily. "Miss Soother, I am not sure that is the wisest idea."

I took a long, deep breath. I was suddenly so angry I couldn't stand it but I somehow knew yelling at this woman wouldn't help my cause. "Do you mind if I ask why?"

"You know your momma worked here for a while?" she said, suddenly much more aggressively.

"Oh," I said, followed by several more long, deep breaths to hold my temper. I remembered Nick next to me, on his back, his bare chest rising and falling, grimacing over me and my mouth. I flushed. "I am not, my mother, Mrs. Mowry. I am rather surprised that you can't see the difference between us. Thank you."

Her mouth dropped open, which wasn't surprising given my tone of voice. I turned on my heel and stormed out of the store. I walked out of view of the front window, and then sat on a curb where she couldn't see me.

I put my head in my hands, and rocked back and forth silently for a few seconds. I had to hold my tongue, I knew. I needed a job. Nick had already asked around on his side of the fence for ways to make money. We needed every cent we could get to get out of here.

Unfortunately, no matter how much I worked to curb my temper, I got the same general reaction in three more places within the next thirty minutes. Now I was angry and humiliated.

I was sitting at the far end of Maple kicking dirt when I heard a loud whistle from the far end of the street. I looked up and my stomach fell. Jimmy Reid was standing in the doorway of one of the older brick homes that lined this end of Maple.

When our eyes met, he half smiled, blew me a kiss, and disappeared back in the doorway. I got up and immediately tore back down Maple Street towards my house, the woods, towards Nick and safety.

I was nearly running by the time I passed back by the deli, and almost collided with Mr. Mowry as he walked out. "Whoa, Menna," he said, gripping me by the arm to keep me from falling. "You OK? Where you running from in such a hurry?"

"Nowhere, I'm sorry . . . I . . . I'm just heading home," I explained, looking back down the street to see if Jimmy was following me. I just saw the normal mid-morning traffic.

"I see," he said, looking down the street and back at my face. The bruise was darker today than it had been yesterday. I couldn't do anything to hide that I had recently been punched in the face. This morning as I got dressed, I had the passing inclination to wait until it healed to attempt this endeavor, but the hope of getting out of here had made me too giddy to wait.

"Someone bothering you?" Mr. Mowry asked. He had let go of my arm and was staring intently at my bruised eye. "I heard you had a bit of a run-in the other night."

"You heard about that?" I asked. I was surprised, since there had been so few people walking towards us as we all scattered away.

He smiled slightly. "It's a small town, Menna, and two of our most prominent citizens are also those that seem to cause the most . . . gossip . . . " I stared at him blankly for a moment, wondering how Max and I could ever be called prominent, before I realized that he meant Jimmy and Emery. "Which one hit you?" he asked finally.

This felt oddly like a trap, like somehow I would utter a name and an officer would jump out from a side street and arrest me for street brawling. I thought again, realizing that I hadn't done anything but run off at the mouth, and Nick was safely away from me right now. "Emery."

Mr. Mowry frowned and nodded in a sad way. "Figures. I don't think Jimmy can hit that hard." He was whispering. I wondered exactly how much influence the mayor had over what was said of his son and nephew, and Mr. Mowry's tone was disconcerting. "Why? Did he see you with that Indian boy you were with?"

I guess all small towns have ears, and I just never thought much of it. It's hard to know what people are saying about you when you don't really talk to anyone. Even at school I kept to myself and remained oblivious to the gossip.

"I guess that's what upset them initially, but I think he hit me because I was sort of mocking him," I said.

"You were mocking Emery?" his eyes were amused and bewildered.

"Sort of, I guess," I said, staring down. "Wasn't the smartest thing I ever did, obviously." I gestured towards my eye.

"Well, I should tell you to go to the police, but I guess that wouldn't really accomplish much," he said. He leaned back against the side of the store and crossed his arms. This was the longest conversation I had ever had with Mr. Mowry, or any of the adults in town for that matter, and I was wondering at what point I would be able to slip away and head to meet Nick. I was devastated to have to tell him how this morning had gone.

Mr. Mowry sighed heavily after a moment, much like his wife had earlier in the day. "Mable tells me you're looking for work," he said.

"I am, sir," I said.

"I don't believe in making a kid answer for what her mother's done, unless that kid is a lot like her momma. Are you like your momma?"

"I'm nothing like her," I said, with more defiance in my voice than I intended.

"You don't drink?"

"No," I said.

"This problem Emery has with you, you think it's out of his system?"

"I have no idea, sir."

He nodded slightly. "Well, Menna, I need someone three afternoons a week to stock shelves and generally clean up. I am willing to give you a shot, but you can't bring trouble into my store. Can you handle that?"

"Absolutely!" I was having a hard time concealing my grin. He smiled back at me.

"And look, Menna, don't take this the wrong way, please, but I imagine that Emery's problem is more with that Indian boy than you, what with him dating your sister, so you just make sure that boy doesn't come around here while you're working, hear?"

I swallowed hard, inhaled. "Yes, sir. When do I start?"

"Tomorrow. Let's say you work two to seven Mondays, Wednesdays, and Fridays, till school starts, then it will be three to eight to give you time to make it here," he said.

"I will see you tomorrow!" I had control over both my smiling and my temper as we said good-bye and I walked away.

I was figuring it all out in my head as I moved towards the hill. Math was the one area I was better in than Max, finally. Fifteen hours a week times, say, forty-five more weeks before we were to leave. I could easily have a couple of thousand dollars saved in time. To me, that sounded like enough money to buy a palace.

Nick was sitting waiting for me. I ran up to meet him, threw my arms around his neck and knocked him to the ground. "I have a job!" I announced before I planted my mouth on his and kissed him as hard as I could. He wrapped his arms around me and rolled over until he was on top of me.

"Congratulations," he said, and then he kissed me.

"I missed you last night," I said when I could breathe, realizing how ridiculous it sounded. I was beginning to remind myself of the giggly cheerleaders in the bathroom at school.

Nick pulled back from me to lay on his side. "Max OK? He looked so spooked yesterday."

I looked away from him, straight to the sky. "He knew."

"Knew what?"

I rolled to face him. "He knew that we . . . well . . . he knew why I didn't come home."

Nick smiled, touched the edges of my bruise with his fingers.

"Nick, you can stop doing that, it's only going to get better. I can see you feeling guilty every time you do that," I said.

"Is he mad?" he asked.

"Max? I don't think so, I don't know. He didn't seem to be. He, well, he asked me what it was like," I said.

"He wanted details?" Nick looked stricken.

"No, I think just a general synopsis."

"What synopsis did you tell him?"

"I told him that being that close to you was the most wonderful thing I've ever felt," I said. I was surprised to get it out without stuttering and faltering and questioning my words.

"I'm glad to know we would both describe it the same way," he said, then laughed a bit. "I'm even more glad that you didn't give your brother a detailed description."

I punched him lightly, and laughed a bit to myself. "We're doing this, Nick," I said. "I will have a couple of thousand dollars by next June. We're doing this!"

"Yeah, we are," he said, his voice full of hope.

Chapter Nine

*T*he porch creaks as Max steps on it. He flinches slightly, but continues on to the door anyway. From the outside, he guesses no one has lived here for years, but then again, he wondered how many people thought that throughout his childhood.

It's funny, he thinks pausing on the porch, how he never noticed that when he was younger. He never saw how rundown his house was, at least not until Lily pointed it out.

Thinking of her, which he has tried not to do for years, he shivers involuntarily, despite the thick, muggy air around him. He shakes off the thought of her.

He reaches to knock, realizes the door is open, and pushes it slightly. The living room is in disarray, empty bottles, broken glass, and debris cluttering the floor. He half smiles and says, "Mom, I'm home."

Of course, no one is there. He knew that before entering, but he stands for a long while in the living room, noticing how many things here are exactly as he'd left them.

Finally, finally, he inhales deeply and heads to the stairs, up to the attic. In the corner, his old typewriter gathers dust. Sheets of paper scatter across the floor. He picks up one, then another, smiling in a pained way over the words he wrote when he was so much younger.

Inside his pocket, his phone buzzes. He retrieves it, stares at the blue-lit screen that tells him Netis is calling. He stands as he answers it, his "hello" ringing of desperation. "Netis?"

"Hi, Max," her voice says, despondent and far away.

"I've been calling and calling since I left," he says.

"I've been reading. I called in sick last night to finish reading," she says.

He closes his eyes, inhales sharply. "So you know then?'

"I know," she says. "What I don't know is why you kept this from me."

"I don't know, Netis, and I'm sorry, I guess I've just always felt like so much of it wasn't my story to tell," he admits.

"It was, Max. After all of these years, I know you now, and I've realized that I never quite understood a lot about you, and now I do," she says.

He thinks back, remembering so many nights when she rested her head on his shoulder and shared her life with him. She had told him, so easily, of things he couldn't say out loud. She had told him about her mother beating her over and over with a cool indifference. He knew her, and when he held her, he knew everything that he had his arms around. But he had never let her see him.

"Where are you?" she asks.

"I am standing in the attic of our old house," he says.

"Oh," she says quietly. "Have you seen your sister yet?"

"No," he says. "I had to come here first, immerse myself in this for a while, get ready."

"OK," she says. She pauses. "Max, are you still coming back?"

He smiles, though the fear in her voice hurts him. "Of course I am. I hope to be back by the end of next week."

"OK," she says.

"I love you," he says.

"OK," she says, and hangs up softly.

Max takes one more survey of the debris around him, and goes back downstairs to the living room, which he barely glances at before moving straight out the door and to his car.

He drives directly to the motel/deli, and notices a car outside with New York plates. He stares at it for a long time before he goes in.

"Mr. Soother," Mrs. Mowry says from the desk. Max remembers her from his sister's summer job at the deli. She had never been this polite, nor smiled at him. Now she beams. "You know, we're all very proud of you."

"Thank you," he says. "I assume my sister is here?"

"Yes," she says cautiously. "Room four. And the child."

Max looks at her, confusion painted on his features. "She has a child with her?"

"Yes," Mrs. Mowry says, and Max wordlessly picks up his key and mounts the steps. He opens the door to room three and sets his small suitcase on the floor before crossing to room four and knocking on the door.

He realizes then how early it is. The sun has barely risen, he had driven straight through the night.

He hears a groan, and feet padding across the floor. The door flies open and a young girl stands before him, fire red hair, and eyes that were troublingly familiar. She is tall, and lanky. She stares at him through one open eye, clearly still thick with sleep.

"Hello," he says. "I'm . . . "

"You're Max, my uncle," she says. Both eyes open, and she sticks her hand out formally. "I'm Cole."

"Cole?" he asks.

"Well, it's Nicole, but I go by Cole."

"Oh," he says calmly.

Max looks beyond her now, and sees Menna standing a few feet back. She has put on a robe, and is standing, arms crossed, a nervous smile playing on her face, behind Cole.

"Max," she says.

"Menna," he says.

"I'm glad you're here."

Max

Typically, school years passed for me in a blur, the space between summers. I loved school, unlike Menna, and I always did well. However, it never took enough effort to do well for school to fully occupy my mind. The library closed early during the winter, and, particularly that winter, with Menna working three afternoons a week and with Nick every other free second, I had no idea how to entertain myself. And so, I began to watch.

There was nothing perverse about it—I wasn't creeping up to my neighbors' windows at night to look in on their private moments. I was following Lily around, observing her interactions with Emery from afar, and trying to learn as much as I could about this dangerous man.

This began in mid-October, as the town families were putting their carved pumpkins out on the steps. I had just stopped into the deli to see Menna. I was seeing her more during the time she was there stocking shelves than I did at home. But on this day she had been grumpy and told me that she was too busy to talk to me. I sulked away.

As I came out on Maple, a glimpse of flame-red hair heading the other way caught my eye. Lily walked a few steps behind Emery, her head down and no sign of the defiance she usually wore. I didn't even think about it before I ducked across the street and began walking about a block behind them. I stuck very close to the buildings, weaving in and out of porches and awnings, but staying near enough that I could always see my sister.

They were heading out of town the opposite direction of our house. A few blocks up, and Emery turned to her, smiled in a leering way, and put his arm around her and they began to walk together.

It wasn't until this moment, ten minutes after I had begun to trail them, that it occurred to me to wonder what I was doing. I hadn't intended to follow them, I just . . . I had to know when he hurt her.

Maple began to grow desolate as it transitioned from the heart of town to a country road. I stayed back even further, letting Emery and Lily remain far in front of me. This far out, a creek ran alongside Maple. It was separated from the road by a long, flat field at least a hundred feet wide and partially obscured by a sparse tree line.

They didn't seem to be speaking to each other as they wandered down by the creek. I crouched by an old tree stump, so far from them that only Lily's hair was visible to me. They sat down on the bank, and after a while I began to creep closer.

I could sense, even from this distance, how different their interactions were from those I had witnessed between Menna and Nick. Emery and Lily seemed anything but natural with each other. While Menna and Nick almost seemed to share a common motivation for each moment, and an inexplicable private gravity that pulled them to each other, Lily and Emery seemed awkward and uncomfortable with each other. I wondered if this was perhaps a product of the amount of time they had spent together—perhaps they had simply grown tired of being so in-sync. Perhaps, Menna and Nick were unnatural, and few couples could strive to seem so at peace when together.

The maniacal urge to observe drew me closer to them. I needed to know if he hurt her, and was troubled by the fact that I couldn't quite tell why. She was my sister, of course, and I was the only man in our house; nonetheless, my feelings towards Lily were as conflicted and confused as her behavior towards me.

I was maybe twenty feet from them when Emery shifted suddenly. I froze, thinking that he had heard me and was about to charge. I was terrified of the prospect of facing down this thick, large man who always seemed to be seething. However, after a moment I realized that he had instead charged Lily, pushing her onto the ground.

She had on a skirt that day, and he roughly yanked it up over her hips, and stripped off her bright white underwear. He laid those next to him, a stunning contrast to the dying leaves on the ground. He kissed her succinctly, once, twice, three times, and then reared up on his knees to unbutton his pants. I looked away for the next few moments, but heard Lily gasp slightly, followed by the rhythmic rumpling of the leaves around them.

After a few seconds, I had to look back. Even now, I remember Lily's face in that moment. She didn't look pained, though she didn't look like she was enjoying it either. Her mouth was set in a firm line, and her eyes closed softly. Lily was simply enduring this.

I found a large stone far away from them and sat, thinking and waiting for the sound of crumpling leaves to end. I was ashamed of myself for watching this, and even more ashamed of the growing doubt I felt. Menna and Nick must have been wrong. While Emery clearly wasn't as gentle or adoring of Lily as Nick was of Menna, he hadn't hit her or even raised his voice to her yet. They had to have been wrong. It have to have been Momma that hit Lily.

This theory, however, only served to further fill me with angst. I couldn't protect Lily from Momma.

And why had Nick and Menna lied?

Even as I thought it, I knew it wasn't *them*, it was *him*. He took Menna's trust and confidence away from me. He convinced me wrongly that Lily was in danger. While Emery certainly was menacing, I had only ever seen him be violent when Menna had provoked him.

Nick had done to Menna what Emery was doing to Lily now. The idea of him, so tall, so powerful, on top of my sister, endurance and impatience painting her face, made me feel sick and angry and hopeless all at once.

I couldn't, however, balance the whimsical and happy tone of Menna's voice when she had told me how wonderful it felt to be with Nick with the look on Lily's face now. But that, too, had to be *his* doing. She believed everything he said, and he had convinced her that she enjoyed this brutal and base act.

The sound of voices pulled me from my thoughts. I began to pay attention as the argument was starting, though it barely progressed past the beginning.

"I already told you, Lily, I gotta meet Jimmy," he said.

Emery was no longer on top of her, and Lily was shaking the debris from her underwear, and trying to slide them back on with whatever modesty she could muster.

"I just thought you were going to take me," she said. I assumed she meant to work. She was now a waitress in the next town over. I always assumed she took the bus to get there, though I had never given it much thought.

"I told you, I am not your fucking chauffeur," he said.

"I know that, Emery, it's just that coming out here has made me late," she said back. I peeked around the rock. As she said this, Emery stared directly at her as he stood above her, fastening his belt. The look on his face was cold, and furious all at once.

"I am sorry," she said, looking down, and that is when I saw it cross her face—fear. Lily was scared of Emery.

I moved away, then, heading along the tree line in a low crouch back towards town. My shame grew—it was a feeling that was becoming all together too familiar to me. I hadn't seen him hit her, but the look on her face, the way the sight of his anger had prompted her to immediately back down, all of it told me unquestionably that everything Nick and Menna had said was true.

Nick wasn't a monster who had stolen my sister from me. He wasn't a liar, a manipulator, a defiler. He was Menna's lover and protector. I was the one who had failed her, and failed Lily.

I decided on the way back to town that I was going to be the brother I should be. I was going to be a man. Menna was fine—Nick kept her so close to him and so safe that I knew I didn't have to worry about her. Lily needed me.

And so, starting that afternoon, I began to watch Lily. I didn't think at the time, and am still not sure, how I imagined I would help her. If her hit her, how could I stop it? He was twice my size and I had never hit anyone in my life. But I felt propelled to do *something*.

Menna

It was late that fall, a cold fall for Alabama, that I walked up the steps to our house, ragged and dirty from my shift at the deli, to find Nick sitting on the steps. Throughout July, August,

September, and October, we had managed to pull together more than a thousand dollars in our relocation fund.

Not that it was easy. School was enough of a struggle for me, and the odd jobs Nick found to contribute to the fund were pulling him away more and more. Several times over the past weeks I had gone to the cottage to wait for him after work and remained waiting until very late before he finally came in, exhausted, and laid down, content to simply put his arm around me and drift to sleep.

Finding him on the porch that night, a place where he always looked slightly odd as though he were somehow too big for the space, was a welcome surprise. Though I spent every spare moment I could salvage with him, I felt myself missing him frequently. When he wasn't next to me, it seemed as though somehow the air around me was broken and inconstant.

"Menna," he said, grinning as I approached. I stopped at the end of the sidewalk just to look at him. He stood up, well over six feet tall, long hair pulled back haphazardly at the base of his neck. It was longer than mine, and thicker, and seemed fitting with his near-black eyes. Looking at him, feeling how immensely content I was to be near him, I was suddenly overrun with an inexplicable sadness. I shook my head, warding it off, wondering where it had come from, and took a step forward as though to escape the moment.

"Hey," I said.

"Go get some clothes," he said.

"What? Why?'

"Just do it," he said.

"I have clothes at the cottage, though after today, what I really want is a shower," I said.

"Shower, but do it quickly. And get other clothes. We aren't going to the cottage," he said, sitting back down and folding his arms in a stubborn way to let me know that he wasn't going to reveal any more.

"You seen Max?' I asked.

"Yeah, he's here. Trailed in after Lily about half an hour ago."

I shook my head. Max had barely spoken to me lately, though not due to anger but because he was so wrapped up in something . . . for once I had no idea what it was. He hadn't been the same since the fair. I didn't know if it was watching Emery hit me, or the knowledge that we were leaving in only six more months, or something else entirely.

"I'm worried, Nick," I said.

He turned his head to face me, a compassionate smile playing on his lips. "We'll talk about it," he said, "I promise. And soon, but now I need you ready to go in . . . " he paused to look at a too-small watch tethered to his wrists, "nineteen minutes." I had never seen him wear a watch before, nor change the subject when he knew I needed to talk to him. I was now intrigued and headed inside.

I showered quickly and assembled the few articles of clothing that remained at the house. Almost all of my stuff was slowly migrating to the cottage. I left much of it there, near where Nick spent his nights, so that when I dressed for school in the morning I still smelled slightly of him.

I wanted to tell him that my worry was based on more than Max; the situation with Emery and Jimmy was escalating. They had been arrested a month before for robbery in the next town. We all figured that they would get a slap on the wrist for this, and they seemed to think the same. This new knowledge that they were invincible meant the time between the arrest and their sentencing left them emboldened. They had been coming into the deli more and more over the the last few weeks Days prior, I had turned from the shelf I was stocking to find Jimmy standing directly behind me.

"Hello, Pretty," he said, running his fingers across my cheek. I slapped his hand away. Emery had walked up beside him.

"Oh, she's a feisty one," he said.

"Like her sister," Jimmy said.

"Like her sister used to be," Emery added. He leaned in close to me. "I broke her of that habit," he said.

"Get away from me," I said, barely whispering. It had terrified me, being this close to the two of them, though the other aisles of the store were crowded.

"You have a lot of pride for an Indian fucker," Jimmy said, loudly enough that the cashier who was working walked over to investigate.

"You two move on," the man told them. I can't remember his name now, this savior, but I remember feeling relief to see him like I had never felt before. Emery and Jimmy left wordlessly.

I thought, again, as I got ready that evening, that I should tell Nick. I had initially decided not to. Nothing had *really* happened, and him knowing would only make him angry, and make him worry. I didn't want him to think he needed to watch me while I was working. I wanted to pass through the next months as quickly and quietly as possible. I needed to keep Nick away from Emery and Jimmy Reid. As I headed downstairs to meet him, I reconfirmed that I had done the right thing in not telling him.

The porch was thick with his anxiety as I stepped outside. I hadn't even looked for my brother. "Did I make it on time?" I asked.

"Yeah, that was only sixteen minutes," he said, taking my hand and leading me out of the yard, up the sidewalk and towards town.

He dropped my hand as soon as we turned on Maple, but stayed closer to me than was typical. "OK," I said, finally. "I've been a good sport. Where are we going?"

"You'll see," he said, grinning. We stopped on the corner across from the deli. A few minutes later, the bus rumbled up, and we got on.

I played along, as we boarded. We moved towards the back, and sat together. It felt somehow rebellious. When, in the darkness, his hand moved over and took mine, it felt dangerous and somehow all the better for its danger.

"Can I know now?" I whispered. We were at least five rows back from the next set of passengers. Over the rumbling of the engine, the whispering was hardly necessary, but somehow it contributed to the overall tone of the outing.

He turned to face me, pushing a stray hair off the side of my face and over my ear. "I love you," he whispered, kissing me so quickly that I barely noticed he had done it until he was gone.

"I already knew that," I said grumpily, though I then leaned my head on his arm and closed my eyes.

I didn't realize how tired I was until the bus rolled to a stop and woke me, which must have been hours later. I looked up startled, and Nick laughed quietly at my expression. "You make for lousy entertainment on the road," he said.

"I'm sorry," I murmured, absently touching his cheek as I looked beyond him outside. We were along a river, and the houses that lined the street looked oddly old-fashioned. "Where are we?"

He grinned as broadly as I had ever seen before. "New Orleans," he said.

I stared at him absently for a moment, and then glanced back out the window. "We're in New Orleans . . . "

He began to talk quickly, as though somehow justifying us being in this place. "You said you had never left Alabama, and we are doing so well with the savings, so I thought maybe I could spend some of mine. I wanted to do something nice for you, and we have a free place to stay here, I just thought . . . " he trailed off as he searched my face desperately for some kind of response.

The only response I could muster was to kiss him quickly and whisper thank you before I stood up and bounded off the bus. He was behind me a few seconds later, his arm twined around my waist, and pointed me down a vibrant street.

"Where's the free place?" I asked.

"Molly," he said. I tried not to trip when he said it, but a feeling of shame spread across me. I hadn't seen Molly since the day on the hill, so many years before. Nick stopped and turned to face me. "She's here for school. She is in town tonight, and then heading out tomorrow so we can stay until Sunday." I nodded slowly. "And she wants to see you."

"Why would she want to see me? I was so terrible last time," my face burned.

"She loves you because I love you," he explained, pulling me close to him. "It'll be fine. Let's go," he said.

Nick pulled me through the streets, which felt electric in a way I couldn't describe. There were people everywhere. I was so rarely in a place where every face was new and unknown. It was terrifying and exhilarating all at once. We were moving so fast through the crowd and I was thankful for Nick's hands pulling me through, otherwise I would have been lost in an instant.

I faintly heard music billowing in around us from many different places, carrying with it the faint smell of smoke and disparate laughter. I stopped again, in front of a long, narrow alley that was lined with buildings covered in flowers and intricate black balconies that looked like flowers.

"What's wrong?" Nick asked. He had to scream into my ear to be heard over the noise.

"Nothing," I said, shaking my head. It was too quiet for him to hear, so I smiled at him instead, and we continued on through the city.

When the music faded out and the laughter began to die down, we found ourselves in front of a small building. It was beautiful in comparison to anything back home, but plain in comparison to everything around it. "This is it," he said, ringing the bell.

A few minutes later, Molly appeared at the door. I remembered her being pretty, but she struck me at that moment. Her thick hair was wound into a loose braid, which trailed over her shoulder. She was dressed simply in jeans and a solid-colored long sleeved shirt, but seemed like she could easily step into the most elegant of settings. She looked amazing, and she looked happy to see us, a wide smile set on her face. She looked like Nick.

"Nick, Menna, so glad you are here," she said, ushering us into a small courtyard. We followed her up an outdoor staircase to a small patio. She opened a door and ushered us into a small apartment.

The front room held only a couch and a table. It opened to a dining room I could see from behind.

She beckoned us to the couch, and then pulled a chair from the dining room table and sat across from us. "How was the trip?"

Nick smiled. "It was long, but Menna slept through it," he said.

She looked at me, her smile never faltering. "Were you surprised?" she asked.

"I was," I said, wondering why I was so nervous. "I didn't know you were in New Orleans. I thought you were up North," I said.

"I'm doing an internship here this semester," she explained, "and then heading north again. I have to go out into the bayou the rest of the weekend, so I suggested to Nick that you come take advantage of a free apartment here. It's a great city," she beckoned out the window.

I nodded and an uneasy silence fell. After a moment, Molly turned to Nick. "Hey, kid, why don't you walk down to the corner? I ordered pizza and you can pick it up," she said.

Nick nodded wordlessly, and went to the door, as though he knew where to go. When it closed behind him, Molly looked steadily at me for a moment before speaking.

"Menna, I know you must be a little overwhelmed, being here. But, I wanted you to know that Nick has been writing me about you, about the both of you, and about your plans. I am happy for you both. I feel like I know you, from his letters," she said.

"Oh, I didn't know he wrote you about me," I said quietly.

"You're all he writes about, you and your plans for going to Maine," she said.

I nodded. "Molly, last time we met . . . " my voice faded, as I realized that I wasn't sure what I had intended to say.

"Last time we met, we were all kids, and now we're all adults," she said. I was seventeen, and it felt odd to be referred to as an adult. Though, I suppose, I was more so than my mother.

"Thank you," was all I could think to say.

"He loves you so much," she said. "It makes me happy. I worry about him, being so sensitive and there alone," she looked past me, out the window as she spoke, as though she had forgotten. Her voice, too, sounded far away.

"I love him, too," I said after a moment of silence, as though defending myself.

"I know," she said. "And I am so glad you are both leaving that place. I was thinking, perhaps, Maine would be nice after I'm a doctor as well. Nick is the only real family that I care about, and I would like to be near you."

"That would be wonderful," I said, meaning it. "I wish we were leaving tomorrow. We almost have enough money. We just need to wait a few more months for me to finish school."

"How is your brother handling this?" she asked.

My face burned. "It's hard to tell. He's always . . . "

"Inside himself?" she asked.

"Yeah," I said.

A rowdy crowd passed nearby on the street, disrupting the quiet around us.

"You like it here?" I asked.

"I love this city," she said. "It's so alive. And where I'm from, where we're from . . . "

"Isn't," I said, finishing her thought with my own.

"And how is it in Boston?" I asked.

She smiled. "I love that city, too. I think you both will love New England. I know Nick will. There are so many places to go and think and be alone, and then you can be in a city around people in a heartbeat."

I smiled. "That sounds like it would be heaven to him."

"And what is heaven to you?" she asked.

"Being with Nick," I said before I thought about it. I was instantly angry at myself for that, for making it sound like *he* was all there was to *me*, although in truth, he was such a large part. But I looked at Molly, successful and independent, beautiful and strong, and realized that I must have looked pathetic to her, like some backwoods little girl who lived only for a man. "And other things, I like the woods, too, and being outside," I offered quickly.

"Menna, it's OK. I know there is a lot to you," she said, as though she had known was I was thinking. "You should look into some schools in Maine, find something you love to do. I can help," she offered.

My apprehension began to fade. She seemed so genuine, and I could believe that she may think of me as something other than the child who ran from teasing years before.

"That would be wonderful," I said.

"I want us to be friends," she said.

"I hope we can be," I added.

Nick came back in, then, a stack of pizza boxes in his hands. "Moll, how many people were you expecting?" he asked.

"I didn't know what you guys liked, so I ordered a bunch of different stuff," she shouted over her shoulder as she walked through the dining room. It must have lead into a kitchen, because she returned a moment later with a stack of plates.

We ate pizza, talked, and laughed for hours. I loved to watch Nick and Molly, who had known each other for their whole lives, speak of shared memories. Nick's life outside of me was something he kept so quiet, so much to himself. Now he spoke openly about parties they had, games they had played. But there frequently seemed to be something left unsaid.

As the night wore on, the noise from the street grew, and Molly looked outside and smiled. "This place comes to life on a Friday night," she said.

"Sounds like it," Nick said, getting up and walking to the window. While it looked out onto a courtyard, the lights from the city beyond the roof were clearly in view. "Hey, Moll, remember when you turned eight and your mom threw that silly party but forgot to make the cake?"

Molly laughed, and looked to me to explain. "She had to go to four or five different places to find one she could buy. So the party didn't start until almost nine o'clock at night."

Nick smiled, staring outside. "It was dead quiet all day, and then there was this burst of activity. We were all running around, and then . . . "

"Then by nine thirty we were all asleep." She was grinning quietly.

"My dad kept trying to wake us all up and make us play, but we wouldn't," Nick kept going. "He was so upset." He suddenly looked a little lost, the smile falling. "He used to bring that up all the time, that when he wanted to have fun, we wanted to sleep."

I had said so little during this time, and still had no idea what to say. I looked at his back, wanting intensely to go to him, and wrap my arms around his waist, but I felt odd doing this in front of Molly. Nick wordlessly turned to face me, and then sat next to me. He didn't put his arm around me, but our legs touched. He smiled again, winked at me, and turned to look at Molly.

"How late are they at it?" he asked, nodding towards the window.

"Late," she said. "I've learned to sleep through it, which is something I should be doing. I'll be gone before you wake up."

She stood and stretched. It occurred to me how uncomfortable she must have been, sitting in the small wooden chair for hours.

"The couch folds out. Let me get you pillows," she said.

I slept next to Nick nearly every night, but it seemed so odd how comfortable she was in the assumption that we would do the same here. It seemed awkward to me, sleeping next to him with her so nearby. He reached over and squeezed my hand briefly as she left the room. He kissed my forehead wordlessly.

Molly returned, two pillows and a blanket in her hands. I couldn't remember the last time I had slept on anything but the floor, be it in the attic or in the cottage. The idea of the bed made the whole situation seem surreal by its very ordinariness. Here we were, visiting a relative out of town, getting ready for bed. This was quiet and comfortable and so unfamiliar.

We opened up the sofa bed, and made it up before Molly shyly handed me an envelope. "A present," she said, "to help with the planning."

"Moll, what did you do?" Nick asked, his voice gently reproachful.

"I want you out of there, Nick, both of you, and I wanted to help," she said. I opened the envelope and found two bus tickets from Mobile to Bangor. They were dated for late June.

"Molly," I said, looking up, "this is too much, we can't . . . "

"You can and you will," she said. "I saved money this summer, too, you know, and I know it's got to be hard working and school and everything."

I knew she wasn't that much older than me, but she seemed so wise and so knowing. Without thinking, I threw my arms around her. She hugged me back, and then extricated herself from my arms and left the room wordlessly.

"Moll . . . thank you, " Nick called after her.

We both stood looking at the envelope in my hands. Though it held nothing but paper, it felt so heavy and so real.

"This is really happening," I said.

"It's you and me," he said, and hugged me as excitedly as I had hugged his cousin a moment before. Though I felt so out of place in this room, this city, suddenly everything seemed so normal. "We just need to make it through a few more months."

The image of Emery and Jimmy Reid standing so close to me at the deli flashed through my head, but I quickly let the sound of the revelers outside, the heat from Nick warming my skin, and the peace I felt being in some other place wash them away.

We curled up together on the small sofa bed. It was uncomfortable, with springs poking into me no matter how I positioned myself. Nick rolled over to face me, and kissed me intently. His hand went to my back, finding the skin under my shirt. I pulled away from him. "Your cousin is in the next room," I whispered, and kissed him definitively.

"I know, Menna. I will be a *gentleman*," he said, smiling as he said the word as though it were dirty. "I'm just so happy, I feel like I can breathe being here."

"I know how you feel," I said, nestling into him and whispered good night before I fell asleep.

But the next night, with Molly gone (leaving an order in the form of a note that we take her bed), tired from hours of exploring, so sated with the feeling of revelry and intoxicated by the charm of the city, I let his hands wander where they wanted.

We tangled together in the large, white bed, with the windows to the courtyard open. The air from the outside, the electricity of the city, flowed over me as we made love. We fell asleep, whispering into the night about how wonderful it would be when we got to do this every night. I felt calm, blissfully calm, and happy in an easy way that was strange and exhilarating.

The feeling stayed with me, carrying me through the bus ride the next day. The closer we got to town, to home, however, the more it faded, replaced by a desperate knot in my stomach and a fear that I couldn't quite explain.

A mile from the edge of town, Nick let go of my hand and separated himself from me by a few inches. When the bus stopped, we climbed off, and headed towards my house, carefully keeping a few inches between us.

There was a crowd of people standing on the corner opposite the deli. They were all speaking intently and excitedly, and I began to walk slowly as we passed, anxious to hear what was being said.

"A year?" I heard one voice say.

"Yes, a year. Not long enough if you ask me," another answered. "Nice to know that we were all wrong in thinking that they would just get away with it."

Another voice added in, "Guess that judge doesn't care who his daddy is."

Nick was ahead of me, outside of the crowd. Everyone was so engrossed in the gossip, that no one looked at either of us with any interest. Finally, the names.

"So where they sending Emery and Jimmy for their stint?"

"Up at the center in Mobile. Maybe a year there will make them boys think a little more before they run around here like they own the place."

I caught Nick's eye. He had heard it, too. Emery and Jimmy were gone. He smiled and winked at me.

It was going to be OK. *Just a few more months.*

Chapter Ten

*M*ax and Menna are sitting on their hill. The sun is high above them, the heat overwhelming. They had found their way to this spot silently, leaving Nicole in the room to sleep. The silence followed them, and they sit quietly for a long time staring out into the woods. Finally, Max speaks.

"She looks like Lily."

"Exactly like Lily," Menna agrees. "Has a little bit of her temperament, too, but she is really quiet most of the time."

"Where is she?" he asks.

"She left when Nicole was two, said she couldn't take it anymore and disappeared," Menna says, her voice flat and clinical.

"So you've been on your own with her since?" he asks.

"Yeah, but we're OK. Every couple of months an envelope of money appears. It's usually only a hundred bucks or so, but I know it's got to be Lily."

Max nods silently, and turns his head to look at his sister's profile. "You look tired, Menn," he says finally.

Otherwise, he thought she looks much like she did when they left. Her face hadn't changed much. She was rounder, somehow, though still very thin, and perhaps a bit softer. Maybe it was defeat and not exhaustion that she wore around her now.

"It took a lot for me to come back here," she says after a long while. "God knows I didn't want to."

"Why did you? Why now?" he asks. There is more of an edge to his voice than he probably intends, and the words fall out like an accusation.

She turns slowly to meet his eyes. "Are you angry that I called you?"

"No," he says.

"Angry that I didn't tell you about her before?" she asks.

"About Nicole?"

She looks annoyed. "Yes, about Nicole."

He thinks for a long moment. "No, I guess I'm not. I would have liked to have been able to help, and maybe to know her, but I am pretty hard to find."

She smiles with genuine amusement. "Yeah, you are, Max. It took weeks to track you down."

"I'm sorry about that," he says. A familiar feeling is filling him slowly. *I failed her again,* he thinks. It was familiar, too, that Menna seemed to know what he was thinking without him saying it.

"Max, obviously I call you when I need you," she says. "It was hard to find you, but not impossible, and you came. I was afraid you might not."

"Of course I came," he says, his voice full of hurt. "I didn't hesitate. I left the next morning and only stopped for one night. I could hear it in your voice . . . "

"I need you," she says, and suddenly looks intently at the ground. *It is defeat,* he thinks to himself. Sadness and failure fill him again.

"Menna, what is happening?"

She stands and looks out to the woods for a moment before turning to face him. Even then, her face betrays that she can't get the words out.

"Do you need money?" he asks.

"No," she says, looking almost annoyed. "No, we're fine. I'm a nurse and I take care of her."

"A nurse?" he asks, his face full of surprise. "You went back to school. I never thought you would set foot in a school again."

She smiles. "I had a kid to take care of after Lily left. I did what I had to do."

Max looks at the ground. "She seems like a good kid."

Menna smiles. "She is. She's smart, and I ride her to make sure she does something with it."

"What do you need, Menna?" he says, shaking his head as though to break away from the diversion.

She produces a piece of paper from her pocket, and looks at it with fear on her face. "She asks me, almost every day, to tell her about this," she says, beckoning to the space around her. "I can't do it. I don't want her to know. I feel so terrible doing it, knowing how we used to wonder who our father was, but I just can't tell her."

Her fingers roll over the paper in her hand over and over. She looks past him as she speaks, a desperation filling her face and her voice. "That's why I've never called you before. It's why I was glad when Lily left me with her. As long as it was just me, and I could try to forget this, then I could keep it away from her."

He nods, catches her eyes, and makes her follow his gaze down to the paper. "I got one of these about a year ago, and we moved. I picked her up and moved her somewhere else. I knew it wouldn't take long to get another one. And I knew if I didn't come to him, he would come for us."

She hands him the piece of paper. He unfolds it, reads it. It looks important and official and he feels her fear emanate from it. "He wants her," he says. "How does he know?"

"I don't know. I was sort of shocked when the first one came. There was no phone call, nothing, just a letter in the mail," she says, sitting again. "I guess I always assumed he was in prison and we were safe."

Max's face turns instantly red as he remembers. "They never pressed charges."

She looks to the ground, nodding slowly. *Defeated.* He feels the need to keep explaining.

"You were gone," he says. "I didn't actually see what happened, I was . . . "

"Knocked out," she says so quietly. She is crying, quietly and privately, tears falling onto their hill.

"There were no witnesses, they said, no evidence that they did it," he says.

"If only Molly had gone to the police," she says.

Max was silent for a moment, and then finally says "She did, the next day. They said the same thing."

She stares at him, anger clouding her eyes, replacing the tears.

"Max," she says, after a moment. "You have to help me. Emery can't have her. She's mine. She always has been. I was lost when we left, and she is the only thing that has kept me going."

The pain is bright on her face. It hurts him to look at her, so he looks down. "Have you talked to a lawyer?" he asks.

She shakes her head in a frustrated way. "Yeah, and she is his. I am not a parent, I am not even technically her legal guardian. Unless we can find Lily, I don't have much of a chance to stop him from taking her."

He looks down at the paper again. "I can't believe he isn't in jail for something else by now, him and Jimmy Reid."

"Jimmy is dead," she says, and can't help but smile slightly. "They told me at the desk when I checked in. He overdosed on something a while back."

"Have you seen Emery?" he asks.

"No," she says. "I've been telling Nicole things all the way down here, about us, about growing up here. I'm trying to leave out as much as I can, but I have to take her to court on Monday and she needs to know why."

He stares out at the woods, watching the leaves more quietly in the breeze. *Nothing has changed here,* he thinks. He looks back to his sister, almost expecting to find her a small child again, looking around despite himself to see if he could find Nick.

"Max," she says, pulling him out of the thought. "Please help me. I don't know what to do. She is all I have. I can't lose her."

He stands now, and turns away from her. It overwhelms him, her voice, her pleading, and the absolute helplessness he feels. The paper weighs his hand down, so official. "I don't know what to do, Menn," he says.

She sobs once, and catches herself, nodding quietly. They remain like this, a terrified tension surrounding the hill. The sun moves higher over them, and the heat becomes offensive. Menna stares at the ground until finally, finally, "Do you know where he is?"

"Emery?" he asks, turning to face her, feeling relieved that the tears on her face have dried, feeling ashamed of his relief.

"No," is all she says, and he pauses, then nods.

"Yes, I do."

"Please take me there," she says, and he offers her his hand and helps her up.

They walk down the hill on the opposite side from where they came, off into the woods. She drops his hand as the trees get thicker, and follows silently.

They wind through and through and through until they are nearing the fence. Right before they come to where the trees give way to a small clearing, he pauses. She walks in front of him.

"Nick," she says, whispering to herself, and staring at the ground, now overgrown with grass and weeds. Max sees the bracelet on her wrist as she kneels down.

Max

That spring, as acceptance letters from a variety of colleges came to me, I felt stuck in each moment in an intense way. Time would not pass for me, and at the same time seemed to be hurdling forward, moving me towards the day when Menna would leave.

I wouldn't be far behind her, I knew, with scholarships from several schools available. They would leave in June, and by mid August I would be gone as well.

My mother was gone, too, I knew, though she haunted the house. Her drunkenness had taken on a passive state, and she rarely spoke. Though I could be sitting in the same room with her, next to her on the couch, it was as though she didn't know I was there.

And Menna was almost already gone. I saw her only on the long bus rides to and from school. She always sat next to me, filling the minutes with idle, empty chatter. It was as though she was afraid to stop speaking, afraid to let me speak, in case I would remind her verbally of what I told her with my silence every moment—I was lost at the thought of her being gone.

Emery and Jimmy Reid had disappeared into the Center up in Mobile seven months before, and so, as time finally pulled me into that June, mere days before my high school graduation and Menna's departure, weeks before I turned eighteen, there was a strange peace over everyone but me. I didn't have to watch Lily, and almost could not have since she had moved into a place in town away from us. I didn't have Menna to keep me company. I had only my own thoughts.

Too much time on my hands—that first weekend in June I decided to go into town and get something for Menna to take with her. Something to say good-bye. Even with the importance of the errand weighing on me, I was loathe to do it and finally allow all of this to become real.

I was in the card store at the end of Maple when a mildly familiar voice said my name. I turned to find myself face to face with Molly, who had grown intensely beautiful since I had last seen her years before. "It is you," she said smiling as I faced her.

"Molly, what are you doing in town?" I stammered awkwardly. Other than Menna I rarely spoke to women. The girls at school seemed vapid and frilly, like touching them might turn them dirty or make them disappear. And none of them were this attractive. My face burned.

"I have the summer off and I came to help Nick . . . " her voice trailed as a panicked look covered my face.

"You're here to help them go," I said, quietly.

She nodded, and then resumed her bright smile. "Menna said you are heading to college this fall. Where you headed?"

"Baltimore, I think," I said. "I enrolled in a school there, so I should be leaving in August."

"You know, you could come with us when we head up to Bangor, stay the summer and then go to school," she offered.

She had said *us*, and I knew then that she was part of the *us*, the world Nick and Menna were running to, and I knew without question that I was not. "I'll think about it," I said. I felt the sudden urge to touch her, put my hand on her shoulder, her face. I pinned my arms to my side as I urgently searched myself for some indication as to why.

"You have a birthday coming, huh?" she asked, stepping around me to look at the rack of cards I had been looking through. "And graduation."

"Yes," I said. I knew I was being terse, bordering on rude, but my concentration was not on what to say, but on how to act around her.

She nodded, and looked at the rack as though it was intensely interesting to her. "Hey Max, why don't we go get a cup of coffee? You can tell me all about what you will be studying in Baltimore," she said. She sounded amused as she said the last word, and I realized with intense embarrassment that I hadn't even been able to say the name of the school. I nodded and followed her out of the store, glad, at least, to be emancipated from this errand.

The momentary buoyancy faded as we stepped out onto the street. I saw a flash of red hair next to us, and immediately recognized Lily standing there. A second later, I realized who she was with— Emery and Jimmy Reid. Instinctively, I reached out and took Molly by the arm and attempted to pull her down the street the other way before they saw us.

"Hey, it's your kid brother," I heard behind me and froze. Molly's face was composed, and she turned with me to see Emery and Jimmy walking to us. Lily stayed behind, her face vacillating between mild concern and extreme disinterest. "And who is the redskin with you?" Jimmy asked. He stepped closer to Molly than either of us was comfortable with.

"I'm Molly," she said, her voice steady and confident. I knew she knew who this was—she had grown up here, too—but nothing about her face, voice, or posture betrayed any concern for the situation. "How are you, Jimmy?" she asked.

"Oh, I'm good," he said, "and you are looking good."

Emery leaned against the wall. He looked bored, but stared intently at me. I couldn't meet his eyes.

"Thank you," Molly said curtly. I recognized in her tone the same resolve I had heard in Nick's years before after the carnival. She was trying to keep this from escalating. "Max and I were just going, but it was nice to have seen you."

As she tried to step away, Jimmy grabbed her arm. "Where you going?" he asked. "You're just too pretty to walk away. Ain't she pretty, Emery?"

"I don't like Indian pussy," Emery said. I looked up to meet his stare. He held my gaze with a daring set to his eyes until I looked away.

Jimmy grinned. "I normally don't neither, but for you, sweetie, I might make an exception."

"Well, that is very kind of you, but I am busy at the moment," Molly said. She calmly but effectively shook her arm away from him and took a step back.

Behind them, the door to the deli opened, and Menna stepped out. She looked around for a moment, and then her eyes settled on us. She suddenly looked very afraid.

"Menna," Molly called out, and walked around Jimmy, pulling me behind her. We moved away from them briskly. When we reached the deli, Molly threw her arm protectively around Menna and we all began to walk quickly towards our house. It wasn't until we reached the end of Maple that I turned around and was happy to see that they weren't following us.

"Shit," Menna said quietly. I was surprised to hear her use that language. "They haven't even been gone eight months, what are they doing back?"

Molly bit her lip. "Must have gotten out early." She absently rubbed the arm that Jimmy had been holding as he spoke to her, as I stood by silently.

"Molly, I'm sorry about what they said," I offered, feeling ridiculous and juvenile even as I said it.

She waved it off dismissively. "I've heard worse. Just don't tell my cousin. He is so damned hot headed about the two of them." Menna nodded in agreement, and then the worry faded from her, and she threw her arms around Molly.

"I didn't know you were coming," she said.

Molly hugged her back. "I wouldn't miss your graduation and the chance to see Nick get the hell out of this place."

The two separated and looked to me, as I stood there feeling awkward and out of place next to them. "I haven't even made it home yet," Molly said. "I stopped into the card shop to mail some things, and ran into Max."

Menna looked at me quizzically. "What were you doing there, Max?'

"Nothing," I mumbled.

She smirked and giggled to herself. "Nick's waiting for me at the hill. Does he know you're coming?

Molly grinned mischievously. "Nope."

"Let's go surprise him," Menna suggested, and we headed towards the trees. As we past our house, I contemplated excusing myself and heading inside, but Menna wound her arm around mine as if silently denying the suggestion.

When we reached the hill, Nick was sitting there with his eyes closed. We were almost to him when he opened them, saw the three of us, and jumped up. He threw his arms around Molly and picked her up, reeling her around in a circle. "What are you doing here?" he asked.

"Came to surprise you," she gasped as he set her down. "You guys only have what, another two weeks here?"

Menna and Nick both beamed. "Less," Menna said. "We changed the date on those tickets you gave us. We're leaving in five days," she said. It hit me. The day after graduation. In five days, my sister would be gone.

We all sat without it being suggested, and began to talk lazily through the afternoon. I wondered, over and over, if either Menna or Molly would mention the encounter in town, or at least warn

Nick about the return of Emery and Jimmy. Finally, as the sun began to set, Molly did.

"So, Nick, just so you don't get caught off guard, Emery and Jimmy are back."

She said it lazily, as though she were commenting on the weather, but Nick bolted upright. In the same motion, his hand went to Menna's and gripped it tightly. Menna responded by sitting up on her elbow and running her fingers soothingly up and down his arm.

"What? They aren't supposed to be back yet," he said.

"Must have gotten out early," Molly said. Her eyes had been closed, but now she opened one and looked at him warily.

"What happened?" he demanded.

"Nothing, we just saw them in town on our way out here," Molly said, closing her eye and letting her arm drape across her face. "Don't worry—you can avoid them for five days."

Nick looked from Molly to Menna, searching her face for confirmation of what Molly had told him. What he found was Menna looking guilty and concerned. She couldn't lie to him. He pulled her towards him, kissed her forehead, and held her for a long moment. I barely heard him whisper, "Just a few more days."

I excused myself a moment later to head home and languish through the next few days. I spent most of them going over and over the same stores in town. I had very little money, which I had earned through writing a few small articles for the local paper, but I felt compelled to get Menna something to take with her. I looked at racks of jewelry, but all she ever wore was the bracelet Nick gave her. I poured through books, but she never much liked to read as I did.

Even on the morning of graduation, I had not yet been able to find anything that I thought would work. In desperation, I picked up a small, leather bound journal and purchased it.

An hour before the bus would arrive to take us, sweating and anxious in our cap and gowns, I was staring at an empty page trying to decide what to write. I wanted to be eloquent, somehow encapsulating everything on the page. She was so important to me, and she had to know. I was sorry I hadn't been able to protect her from more of this life, and I needed her to know that. I was always going to be thinking about her, worrying about her, and missing her. But I couldn't put it into words.

Finally, I wrote:

Menna,

You are my best friend, always. You know how to find me if you ever need me. I will do whatever I can to keep you safe, no matter what.

Max

It seemed pathetic and desperate. I angrily shut the book as I heard Menna calling for me downstairs. Together, we walked to the bus and headed towards school.

We sat together silently through the bus ride, which was eerily formal in comparison to Menna's nervous chatter throughout the previous months. She stared straight ahead, and every now and then I would catch her with a smile playing on her lips. We were almost to school when I turned to her and asked, "Are you happy, Menn?"

She seemed startled, and then grew very serious and simply nodded her head.

We got to school and took our places, marched with our classmates, and sat solemnly through a variety of speakers and awards. Menna sat next to me, looking pensive and anxious all at once, but never saying a word.

When finally, at the end of the ceremony, they called our names to walk across the stage, Menna went first and I followed. I shook the principal's hand, and finally looked around at the audience. It was a small crowd, maybe a hundred people—not surprising since there were only thirty in our graduating class—and I saw many faces clearly. In the first row behind the graduates sat Nick and Molly, both looking as though they were about to burst with excitement.

Five rows or so behind them, I saw the red of Lily's hair, and noticed with absolute dread that Emery and Jimmy were with her.

I went down the steps at the side of the stage, and found Menna waiting for me. "I saw them, too," she whispered, and from her tone I knew she meant Emery and Jimmy.

The ceremony ended, and the crowd, sweaty and stiff, rose to its feet and began milling around offering half-felt congratulations to us all. I stripped off my cap and gown and stood, in my best clothes, apart from the crowd watching the interactions. After a moment, Menna came to stand with me.

"What are you doing over here by yourself?" she asked, scanning the audience, presumably looking for Nick.

"Just watching," I said. Emery, Lily, and Jimmy were standing and talking at the back of the field.

Nick and Molly found us then. "Congrats, guys," Molly said, hugging us both. Nick stood apart from her and from us. I could tell by the friction in the air that he wanted to hug Menna but was always wary of doing so in a crowd. "Where should we go celebrate?"

"Let's go out to dinner," Menna suggested, and she and Molly began chattering about plans.

I watched as Lily, Emery, and Jimmy broke away from the crowd and headed off the field, in the opposite direction from the parking lot.

"Max?" Nick's voice called me back to our group. "We were going to go to that diner. You ready?"

I glanced past him at Lily's red hair fading in the distance. I had to follow them. "You guys go ahead," I said. "I have something I need to do."

"Max," Menna said, her voice alarmed. "Please come."

I reached into my back pocket and withdrew the journal. I handed it to her. She attempted to open it, but I put my hand over hers to stop her. "There is something I need to do," I explained gruffly. "I'll see you guys later. Meet you at the hill at ten or so?"

She nodded gravely and watched me go. I wound my way through the crowd, trying to catch up to the trio I needed to follow.

Menna

We had every intention of going to dinner after my graduation, Molly, Nick and me, but as we neared the diner Molly excused herself from us inexplicably, with a knowing smile. Nick turned to face me. "You hungry?" he asked. I shook my head.

Silently, he took my hand and we wandered towards my house. The book Max had given me, one I hadn't been able to make myself open, was tucked into Nick's back pocket. We didn't speak about why Emery and Jimmy had been at my graduation. I almost hoped that we wouldn't need to. We were leaving in a matter of hours. We were almost free.

As we walked into the woods, the reality of it began to consume me. So soon, I was leaving this place with Nick, for good. We were heading north to be together. What came after, we hadn't quite figured out yet, but it somehow didn't seem important. We had pooled our money the night before, left it tucked away in a corner of our cottage. Almost $5,000 seemed like a small fortune to us both. We were going to be OK.

But it being so close was also somehow scary to me. I wasn't scared of going—I wanted to desperately—but the hours between now and when we boarded that bus, crossed the state line and left Alabama seemed perilous and long.

Finally, no more than a five minute's walk from our cottage, Nick turned to face me. "Menna, what should we do when we get to Maine?" he asked.

I smiled. "Find a place to live and a job, I guess."

"No, I mean about you and me," he said.

I was confused. "What do you mean? What about you and me? We'll get a place together and live together and be together."

"Oh," he said quietly, looking sad.

"Isn't that what you want?" I asked, concerned and confused now.

"No," he said. My heart sank and a wave of panic washed over me.

"What?" I asked, trying to keep my voice steady. He met my tone with laughter.

"Sweetie," he said, wrapping his arms around me, "what I mean is that I hope, after you're officially eighteen, we can get married."

I swallowed hard. "What?" I said again. My voice was hoarse and shocked.

He tensed. "If you don't want to . . . "

I freed myself from his grasp, and threw my arms around his neck, pulling him to my face. I kissed him hard and desperately. He responded quickly, pulling me tight against him. Without realizing it, we backed up until he was leaning back against a tree. Finally, he pulled his mouth from mine, and ran his lips across my neck. "You don't want that?"

"Of course I do," I said, and he kissed me full on the mouth again.

When Nick had said, nearly a year before, that we were supposed to learn together, he had been right. There was no awkwardness between us now, we moved quickly in unison. I had learned, in that time, how and when to move with him, and when to move against him, where to touch him and many ways to make him smile, or gasp. We moved easily together now. Nick slid down the tree until he was sitting, me on his lap. He pushed his hands up under my dress, moving my underwear aside deftly as I reached for his belt.

We had never done this outside before, or anywhere other than Molly's place in New Orleans, or the cottage. I didn't care that it was the middle of the afternoon, and that we really weren't *too* far from the edge of the woods, I didn't care about anything but the two of us.

As he pushed into me, I felt both instantly wonderful and suddenly afraid. The nervousness that had plagued me all day escalated to a frenzy. Soon this moment would be over. Soon we would have to leave the woods and walk into town in the middle of the morning and get on a bus together. I focused on that moment , on hearing the engine rumble to life and seeing Maple vanish behind us. I waited, hoped that the image would make this feeling go away, but it only grew.

I wrapped my arms around Nick and held him as close to me as I could, so tightly that I shook from the strain. "Please," I said into his ear, not knowing what I was asking him for. My voice sounded frail and frightened, so very out of place with the way I should have sounded as we made love in the forest. "Please," I said again and then again, feeling the first tear roll down my cheek.

Nick stopped moving, and put his hands on my back to hold me closer to him. "Menna," he whispered in my ear. "Menn," he said, then trying to pull away from me slightly so he could see me. "Menn, look at me."

I slowly convinced myself to let go and move just a few inches back from him so I could see his face. The air rushed in to fill the void I had created between us. Though it was overwhelmingly hot, I shivered, steeling myself against the urge to move back to him and hold him again.

"Menn, whatever you're asking me for, you can have it. You can have anything. We're leaving here in less than twelve hours," he said. Not having any idea as to why, I felt myself began fully cry. Hot tears spilled down my cheeks. I was both shocked at myself and desperate to once again close this monumental gap of inches that had opened between us.

"Menna, please, please, tell me what's wrong," he said, his voice concerned. I sniffled, and kissed him, and forced myself to finally stop crying. I put my hand on the side of his face and looked intently at him.

"Don't ever leave, Nick," I said.

"Why would you even say that?" he asked. By his face, he was confused, and perhaps even a little insulted.

"I'm just scared," I said. "I don't know why. I'm so scared."

Nick pushed the hair back off my face with both hands and met my eyes. "A lot is happening. I guess it's normal to be scared, but as far as me leaving, don't ever even worry about it. I love you. I love you so much. It's you and me."

I kissed him again, more softly this time, and he rocked forward until I was on my back and he was on top of me, and we moved together until we were both spent, and tired and just laid, staring at the treetops.

"You OK?" he asked me, rolling on his side to hover over me.

"Yeah," I said, shaking my head slightly. "I am so sorry, I have no idea what brought that on." But even now, even with him right beside me, I felt like I was falling, like he was disappearing. I inched closer to him. "But I need to be near you."

He gestured to my body on the ground, practically under his, and smiled. "You're pretty near me, Menn."

"Oh," I said, embarrassed by his teasing and a little embarrassed by my own actions.

"Don't get offended," he said, "I know how you feel. On the few nights you don't come and sleep with me, I wake up panicked sometimes, looking for you. I feel like there is an itch in my head until I see you again."

I touched his chin, my hand limp and covered with dirt. "It's hard to believe, only twelve more hours."

"And then..." he rolled onto his back, gathering me against him with his arm. "I looked up some motels in the Bangor area."

"Motels?" I asked.

"Well, yeah, we got so tied up with getting there, that we sort of forgot to plan for what happens when we do," he said. "So I found a few motels that aren't too expensive. I think we can stay in one of those for a few days, until we find a permanent place."

"I've never stayed in a motel," I said, putting my chin on his shoulder. "And I am glad one of us is thinking ahead. I hadn't gotten that far. All I know is that twelve hours from now, we're on a bus. We transfer in Mobile, stop at every town in between here and Maine it seems, and then we're in Bangor sixty hours later."

"Sixty hours, on a bus . . . " he said quietly.

"It'll be fine for me, I'll probably sleep the whole way," I said, rolling back onto my back and stretching. Nick smiled, rolling on top of me and leaning inches above my face.

"We're so close," he said. He buried his face in my neck, and I entwined my arms around his neck.

"Hey, sweetie?" I asked, hoping my voice sounded absent and unconcerned.

"Yes?" he asked, and I felt his breath along my collarbone.

"Do you think it was like this for them?"

He moved away from me slightly. "Like what for whom?"

"Our parents. Did they feel this way, ever?"

Nick put his head down on my chest, and reached out to pull my arms around his shoulders. "I don't know, maybe."

"How could they have stopped?" I asked, absently.

"What do you mean?" he asked.

"I can't imagine ever leaving someone that I loved as much as I love you," I said. "Then again, I can't imagine anyone loving my mom this much. But still, I wonder how they let it fade, if they ever had it." I was more speaking to myself, and Nick, lulled by my voice, by the rising and falling off my chest, closed his eyes.

"Let's make a deal," he said drowsily. "If either of us ever starts to think this is fading, let's have hot sex in the woods and we'll find it again."

I laughed out loud beside myself, and let my eyes close as well. We slept then, as the sun set, on the dirty forest floor. When I woke up, it was dark. The first thing I thought was *how many more hours*? And then I realized that something was wrong. Nick wasn't near me anymore. He was standing a few feet away, staring into the woods.

"Nick, what's wrong?" I asked, sitting up and realizing how stiff I was from sleeping on leaves, bark, and dirt.

He turned to me and put his finger over his lips. I could barely see his face, but could sense from the way that he was standing, that he was listening, rigid, and concerned. A second later, a woman's scream tore through the woods. I was on my feet and next to him in seconds.

"I think it came from over there," he said, and took my hand and we wandered out into the woods towards the cottage. A moment later we heard someone running past us, maybe a hundred yards away. From the other direction, I began to hear a stifled noise, and as we came upon the cottage, I recognized it as someone crying.

I was frozen in place, both hands clamped onto Nick's arm, terrified to let go, to let him step away from me towards whoever was making that noise. I wanted to stay there, holding on, until it was time to go to the bus.

Nick was scanning the clearing. Finally, he said, "Hello?" quietly.

"Nick?" came the garbled response, and from the other side of the house, Molly emerged. As she approached, I was able to see blood dripping from her nose and down her face. The beautiful white dress she had worn to the graduation was dirty and torn. She was almost upon us when I saw the blood trickling down the inside of her legs.

"Oh my God," I said, and Nick dropped my hand and went to her. A moment later, Max appeared from the forest, his chest heaving and sweat pouring over his face. He looked at us, and then at Molly, and just said, "No!"

Chapter Eleven

C ole is playing with her dinner, more interested in staring across the table at Max than she is with eating. A thick silence has pervaded for nearly five minutes. Menna finally sighs inwardly and speaks.

"Cole is not a fan of Southern cuisine."

Cole flips over her untouched piece of chicken fried steak. "I don't call this 'cuisine.' "

Max smiles. "I wondered why you would have ordered that. I grew up in the South and I hate chicken fried steak."

Cole shrugs. "Curiosity. I wanted to know if it was chicken or steak."

Max and Menna both laugh. "You know sweetie," Menna says, "I could have answered that question without you ordering it."

"Some things you have to experience for yourself," Cole shoots back. She turns to Max, setting her shoulders determinately. "So, Uncle, what do you do?"

Max meets her eyes, his expression unchanging. "A lot of things. I work in a bar sometimes, and I write."

"What do you write?"

"Anything someone pays me to write," he says. He picks up his fork.

"So you don't write books or anything?"

"Sometimes," he says.

"You sure don't say much," Cole mumbles.

"Cole," Menna chides.

"What? I just want to know," the girl says, pouting.

"I'm sorry, Cole," Max begins. "What do you want to know?"

Cole thinks, and Menna can tell by her expression that she is about to say something troublesome. Menna inhales as Cole asks, "Do I remind you of my mother?"

Menna groans, but Max doesn't react. "You look like her," he says slowly. "You look a lot like her, but you don't act much like her."

"Did you like my mother?" Cole asks.

"No," Max says quickly. Menna elbows him in the ribs.

Cole thinks for a minute, and then smiles. "I like knowing that you're honest."

"Usually am," Max says. "And what about you? What do you do?"

"I go to school, and do homework" Cole says. "Menna and I go exploring and see all kinds of stuff."

"You like Maine?" he asks.

"I've never been to Maine," she says.

Max turns to look at Menna. She stares down. "I couldn't go to Maine. Not without . . . We stopped in New York and just sort of stayed. First in Buffalo, and then, as of last year, in Albany."

The silence falls again until Cole asks, "So why are you both here? Menna's been telling me about you guys growing up. Did you come to help with that?"

Max again looks sharply at his sister, who shoots him a sideways, helpless glance. "No," he says. "I'm sure Menna tells that better than I do. I came to visit my mother's grave." He tries to continue with his blank expression, but the lie paints his face.

"Grave," Menna says quietly.

175

"She died eight years ago," he tells her. "The house is ours, now."

"I don't want it," Menna says.

"I didn't figure you would," he says. "I've just been paying the taxes. I still don't know what to do with it."

"Can I see it?" Cole asks.

"No," Max and Menna say in unison. Max's voice softens and he adds, "I was there this morning, it isn't safe."

Cole rolls her eyes. "So my grandmother is dead, my uncle isn't here to see me, and this place fries their steak in chicken batter. I hate this place." She says the last sentence quietly, but emphatically. Menna stares at her in disbelief, and with guilt. Max, after a second, begins to laugh.

"Well, now I know we're related. I've always despised this place, too."

Cole smiles, despite herself, and begins another battery of questions.

Max's phone rings, and he drops his fork and attempts to fish it immediately from his pocket. He answers it. "Netis?" A voice sounds on the other end, and he jumps up and heads to the front of the diner.

"Who's Netis?" Cole asks Menna.

"I don't know," Menna says.

"Sure seemed excited to talk to her," Cole comments, and gingerly cuts away a piece of her steak and chews it slowly and quizzically.

Menna doesn't say anything in response, but looks out the window instead. Then, she hears the voice. "Shoulda told me you two were getting in early," and her head shoots around. A second later is she on her feet, positioning herself in front of the booth where Cole sits.

"Go away, Emery," she says emphatically. "You'll see her Monday, not before."

"She looks just like her momma," he says. He looks much the same, though most of his muscles have given way to softness, and a speckle of gray paints his hair.

"I said go away," Menna says again. She feels Cole leaning forward behind her to see this man, visible only in the triangle made by Menna's arm planted firmly on the table.

"You can't keep me from her," he says, cocking his head to the side to meet Cole's eyes. "Judge says you can't."

"How did you even know about her? Why now? Why suddenly care now?" Menna spits.

Emery grins broadly. "Your sister told me," he says. "She came through town about two years ago. Looks really rough."

"My mother was here?" Cole asks, rising to her knees on the booth and peering over Menna's arm.

"Yeah, kid, told me all about you. About how your aunt here made her name you after that Indian," he says, turning his gaze to Menna.

"Go away, Emery," Max says, walking up to the table. He is calm and composed.

"Ah, the kid brother who couldn't speak," Emery says, looking at him.

"I speak just fine," Max says, "and Menna is right. The judge doesn't say anything until Monday, so for now, Cole's guardian has asked you to leave."

Emery turns and stares at Max. "I liked you better when you cowered," he said.

"Sorry to disappoint," Max says, and Emery steps closer to him. Max, instinctively, steps back. Emery smiles and walks by Max and out the door. Max and Menna look at each other warily. Menna sits down, shaking all over.

"Who was that?" Cole asks. They both look away from her. She looks pleadingly from one to the other, and then slumps back into her seat. "Fine. Who's Netis?"

Max looks up. "My wife."

Menna turns to stare at him. "Your wife?"

"Yes," he says, and his composed look withers to a doubtful frown. "She was calling from the airport in Mobile. She's on her way here."

Max

After many hours of moving aimlessly about town from place to place, the trio I was following headed down Maple towards the woods. Lily separated from Emery and Jimmy at our house. I was a block behind them. I watched them disappear into the trees, and stayed back. Lily had looked upset when she headed to the house, but I felt the need to stay with Jimmy and Emery. They had both been drinking, I assumed, from the paper bags they had procured immediately after graduation and took frequent gulps from.

I waited a few minutes and then followed them into the woods. It was nearly dark, and try as I might to silently keep up with them, I quickly lost them.

I had been through these trees so seldom in the past years. What was once a familiar path quickly felt foreign and frightening to me, but I kept moving, always listening for their voices, or the sound of a breaking branch.

After nearly half an hour, I had to admit that I was lost, and had lost them. I must have been the worst follower in the world, and the shame of it kept me moving. I was supposed to meet Nick, Menna, and Molly at the hill at ten. It was barely past eight when I heard the scream. My first thought was Menna—had they found my sister in the woods alone. Would Nick have left her alone? If only I had followed closer and been less afraid of being caught.

I took off in the direction of it, tearing through the woods. Far to my right, a few minutes later, I heard Emery and Jimmy, laughing and belching, heading out. I moved farther left and kept going towards the scream.

Finally, the woods cleared away in front of a small, worn down looking shack. As I broke through the trees, I saw Nick and Menna, her hands wound tightly around his arm. He moved from her and then I saw Molly, covered in blood, her eyes wide and stunned. "No," was all I could think to say.

Nick moved carefully and slowly towards her. "Molly," he said, his voice tight, "what did they do?"

She looked at him for a long time, shuddering every time he stepped closer, until she finally put her hands up. "Stop, Nick. Just stop." She began to shake all over, sobbing softly, looking from one of us to the other. Her knees seemed like they would collapse beneath her at any moment.

Menna crossed to her quickly, and put her arms around her. She whispered into her ear something I couldn't hear, and Molly collapsed against her. The two of them fell together to their knees, with Molly clinging to Menna and crying.

Nick stood behind them with a look I had never seen before. It wasn't rage, or confusion, or even sadness. It was helplessness. Seeing it on his face made me feel lost. He looked to me and quietly asked if it was *them*.

Menna's head shot up and she met my eye. She stared at me, desperation filling her, and I wanted to say it wasn't, that I didn't know. But I did, and I couldn't lie to him, and I knew she really didn't want me to. She just wanted it not to be true.

"Yes."

The helplessness faded, and Nick began to quake. He turned around and punched the side of the cottage. There was a dizzying crack, and I knew from where I stood that he must have broken his hand. He leaned against the wall, his head resting on his arm for a long time. Finally, almost inaudibly, he said, "Molly, I promise you, I will kill them."

"No, you won't," she whispered. "You will get on that bus with Menna tomorrow, we all will, and we will all forget this."

He whirled to face her, walked to her and knelt beside her. Menna was soothingly pushing hair from Molly's face. "We can't," he said. "I won't."

"Please, Nick," she said. "Please, we have to just leave."

"Molly, we have to get you to the hospital," Menna said quietly. She reached out to put a hand on Nick's arm. He brushed it away, and she looked at him with a flash of shock and hurt, which quickly dissipated as she turned her attention back to Molly.

"I'm not going to the hospital," Molly said with steely reserve.

"Which one of them was it?" Nick asked, standing. He was so tall, and seemed even more so standing above the two of them as they sat on the ground.

"Jimmy," she said. "Emery just stood there." She choked as she said his name. "I went into town to get some things, and I came here. I thought you might be here, but you weren't. So I waited, and then the two of them came through the trees . . . "

Menna moved across from her, looking her fully in the face. "Molly, you have to go to the hospital, and then to the police."

"Why?" Molly demanded. "So they can tell me that there is no evidence? So the mayor can show up and try to convince me I imagined this? Or that I asked for it?"

"We won't let them, I promise. We'll stay with you," Menna said.

"The only place I am going is to my mother's house. And you three are all going to your house. I am going to meet you there in the morning, and we're all leaving together," Molly said.

"No!" Nick said forcefully.

"Nick, you listen to me," she said, getting to her feet. Molly was tall, but now she seemed so small and shaken. "You are the only family I have left worth having. You will *not* do anything other than meet me at the bus stop tomorrow."

"Molly, look what they did . . . " he said. He was crying now, hot tears falling over the wide plain of his dark cheeks.

"I know what they did," she screamed. "And they did it to me, *not you*. You let it go, so help me, you fucking let it go." She hit him square in the chest with her balled fist. He stumbled back, and then stepped forward again to wrap his arms around her before she once again fell.

Menna stood up and came to stand next to me. She reached for my hand, held it tightly, and looked at me with some insane hope that I knew what to do. I had nothing to give her, so we stood together for a long time and watch Nick and Molly cling to each other and cry.

"Molly," I said. I didn't know what else I could say, but she looked up at me with the same hope Menna had in her eyes. "Menna is right. We don't know how badly hurt you are. You have to see a doctor." Menna squeezed my fingers.

"I'll be all right tonight," Molly said. She stepped away from Nick and nodded resolutely. "We have to switch buses in Mobile. We'll get off there and I will go to a doctor."

"What about the police?" Nick said. His voice had softened, but I could still hear his anger.

"No," she said. She looked at the ground as she spoke, as though she was figuring it out as she said it. "

"Please," Nick said. Pain filled his voice and he began to cry in earnest. "Molly, please, I can't let them do this."

She put her hand against his lips to silence him. "It's already done. And I want it, I want all of *this* to just be over."

Menna dropped my hand and walked to him, and the three of them huddled together. I stood and watched them. I had been too late again. Finally, they pulled apart. Molly turned to me. "Max, will you walk me home? I want Nick to take Menna home. You meet them there and then you all stay put."

I nodded, and she reached for my arm. I steadied her, and we walked away from Nick and Menna into the woods. Nick kept crying until we were too far away to hear it anymore.

"Max, you have to keep him from doing anything stupid," Molly said to me when we approached the fence. "You have to. This is important."

"I don't understand how you're so worried about all of us right now," I told her, and she nodded thoughtfully.

"I need him, he needs her, she needs you, so worrying about all of you is worrying me," she said. "People have survived worse, Max. Trying to make anyone in this town believe me would be worse."

She found an opening in the fence and turned to look at me. "I'll be fine from here. Hurry home. Please, please hurry. Keep Nick there, and I will meet you in the morning."

I watched her disappear through the fence and into the midst of the house huddled there. I felt heavy and sad, but turned quickly to head home. She had asked me to keep everyone safe and finally, finally, I was going to do it.

I tore back through the woods, somehow finding my way to the hill, over it and beyond, and through the thick woods. The closer I got, the faster I moved, propelled by an intense need to get home. As I neared the field, I saw Menna's tiny form standing in the middle, and I heard shouting. She broke into a run and I followed her.

Menna

For a long time after Molly and Max disappeared into the woods towards the fence, Nick clung to me and sobbed. "Nick, it isn't your fault," I said over and over, wishing that some amount of repetition could make him believe that it was true.

"If I had been here, if we had made it here . . . " he said finally.

"We didn't know she was here," I said. "She was supposed to meet us at the hill. This is no one's fault but theirs."

He stepped back from me, a sudden and eerie calm spreading over him. "I'm supposed to take you home," he said. "You should go inside and get the tickets and the money." I reached for his arm, but he moved away from me.

I did what he said, pulling out the wad of moist cash and two bus tickets, worn from being held in our hands far too often, and clutched them to me. I went back outside. As soon as I neared Nick, he moved forward into the woods.

I followed him, trying desperately to keep up, wanting desperately to touch him, soothe him, do anything to make this better. I had no idea what to do, though, so I just followed silently. When we made it back to the hill, he paused at the top, and turned to me. A half smile crossed his face. "This is the last time we will see this place," he said.

I was suddenly intensely sad. We both looked around for a long moment, silently recalling countless afternoons spent here. "I fell in love with you here," he said.

I finally stepped up to him and took his hand. "Fall in love with me in Maine," I said. He nodded, and we headed down the slope, and into the trees. As we left, I cast a look over my shoulder at our hill, bright with the moon. Despite the darkness, I could almost see him, a boy of eleven, sitting there waiting for me.

And then the trees grew thick, and the hill disappeared from my sight.

We were nearly to the field by my house when he stopped again. We both stood silently, and then I heard what had prompted him to stop. Voices. Laughter. The sound of Jimmy Reid and Emery on my porch.

Nick was instantly tense. "Let's go back," I said. "We can meet Max at the hill and stay in the cottage tonight."

"I can't go back there after what they did there," he said. I grew dizzy at the thought of it. Our cottage, our place, countless mornings spent whispering and laughing, all made ugly now by *them*.

He took a step forward, and I grabbed his arm and held it as hard as I could. "You promised Molly," I said. "You promised me. Please, Nick, don't go out there."

"I can handle myself, Menna," he said, his voice dripping with disgust.

"There are two of them, drunk, and one of you." I said. I was nearly in tears now. "Nick, no, Nick, please no," I said, pulling on him as he took another step forward. He stopped, turned to face me.

"I love you," he said, and kissed me. I leaned into him, wrapped my arms around his waist and held on. Finally, he broke from me and pushed my arms away. "And I am sorry." He ran from the trees out into the field. Halfway across he stopped, and they saw him.

I stepped out behind him, walked halfway out into the field and watched him walk defiantly towards them.

"Hey there, redskin," I heard Jimmy call to him. "I'm having a hell of a time with your kind tonight."

Jimmy and Emery moved from the porch to the street. I was shocked to see Lily run out and stand in front of them. "Guys, no," she said. "Let's just go."

"Get out of the way, Lily," Emery said, stepping close to her. "I think that Nicky here wants to talk to us."

"I'm not here to talk to you," Nick said, his voice filled with rage.

"Nick," Lily said sharply. I can't remember if she had ever said his name before.

"Lily, you need to get out of here now, take Menna and go," Nick said to her.

"I don't much like you talking to my girl like that," Emery said. "I think I may have to teach you your place again."

"Emery, no," Lily said, and he back-handed her across the face and knocked her to the pavement. Nick charged him, knelt forward, and shoved his shoulder into Emery's stomach with all of his might. Emery flew backwards and hit the pavement with a wet thud.

I ran towards them, watching as Jimmy stood, looking helpless and confused. Nick turned towards him, and Jimmy laughed maniacally. Suddenly, Max was beside me, and then in front of me. He ran for Jimmy and hit him as hard as he could. Jimmy stumbled backwards, and then reeled forward and punched Max across the face with his closed fist. Max immediately went down, his eyes closed.

"You're going to pay for that, fucker," Emery said, standing to look at Nick. He took a step towards Nick, who blindly swung and caught Emery in the side of the head.

I knelt beside Max, who was unconscious and watched Jimmy step towards Nick. Nick turned to face him, and punched him in the stomach. Jimmy fell, cursing and sputtering angrily. Nick turned back to Emery just in time to get a fist in his shoulder. He winced, and then swung again.

I watched the fight unfolding in front of me, and instinctively stood to do something to try and stop it. Nick was bigger than both of them, but with the two of them at once, he was getting hit a lot, and I could see him starting to falter. As I stood, I felt a hand on my arm, holding me back, and turned to see Lily. She looked terrified, and just shook her head. I shrugged her off, and moved towards Jimmy.

He stood, and met my eyes. He reached behind him, and pulled a knife out of the waistband of his pants. I stepped back without thinking about it.

"Nick, watch out," I screamed, but before he could turn to face me, Emery punched him and he fell to his knees. While he kneeled there dazed, Jimmy moved behind him and buried the knife in his back.

Nick didn't make a noise. He just turned to look at me, his eyes wide, instinctively reaching behind him and pulling the knife out. Emery and Jimmy both stepped back, turned, and ran. Lily stood to watch them go, and then looked from me to Nick in disbelief.

"Menna," she said, as I stood shakily and moved forward to cover the few steps between me and Nick. He stared at me as I moved, and then fell quietly backwards. Blood seeped from around him onto the pavement.

I dropped the crumpled money and the bus tickets onto the ground, and knelt beside him. He looked up at me, his eyes full of fear for just a second. "Nick," I said, pulling his head into my lap. Instantly I was covered in his blood. "Nick, please, please, please." His mouth moved as though he was trying to speak, but no sound escaped. I leaned down and kissed him softly. "I know," I said. Whatever he was trying to say, I knew he had to be quiet. "Just be still, we'll get help. Be still. I love you, be still."

His eyes grew wide for a second, and he lifted his hand towards me. He never reached me, though, before it fell back to the pavement and he was gone.

Lily was across from me. She picked up the crumpled bills, the bus tickets, and stared at me in disbelief. "You were going to leave," she said.

I nodded before the sob that was growing in my chest overtook me and I screamed as loud as I could. I clung to him, trying to pull his arms around me, kissing him, whispering to him, begging him to shake his head and to get up and to be OK. He didn't respond, his body still in my lap.

Lily stood looking at me for a long time, not saying a word. I couldn't stop looking at him, suddenly seeming so peaceful, couldn't stop begging him to wake up and hold me. Blood smeared the side of his face, and I was also covered in it. I closed my eyes, imagining that this was different. I wished we were on the hill, that

I was cradling his head in my lap as he made plans for Maine and we daydreamed about being together in a big, white bed by the ocean. "Please, Nick," I said one final time before looking up to meet Lily's eyes. She was crying.

"Menna, I am so sorry," she said, her voice choked with sobs. "I am so sorry."

"He's gone," I said. She nodded. "He's gone," I said again, and then "No. No. No. No. No. No."

"I tried to stop it," she said. She glanced behind her at Max, on the pavement. I watched his chest heave. He was OK, but his head would hurt in the morning.

"We told him to stay away," I muttered, pushing hair back off his forehead.

"What did they do?" she asked.

"Molly . . . they hurt her . . . " I said.

"Who's Molly?" she asked, and I stared at her with disgust on my face. She knew so little of my life. I looked back to Nick, and felt sobs overtake me again.

From Maple heading towards us, we heard the sirens. Lily leaned beside me. "Menna, we have to go," she said.

"No," I said.

"Menna," she put her hand on my shoulder, my face, forced me to look at her. "The police are coming, Menna, someone must have heard the yelling. We can't be here."

"We have to tell them what happened," I said.

"They'll know," she promised. "Max will tell them." She looped her arm through mine and tried to pull me up. I pushed her away as savagely as I could, looked back to Nick, pushed the blood-matted hair off his forehead. I stared at his mouth, and closed my eyes again. Again, I imagined his voice telling me what the beach would be like, and the trees. I imagined him reaching for me, and the sadness at knowing he was gone hit me. I began to shake all over.

"Menna, please, we have to go," she said. "There's a bus to Mobile in half an hour. Let's get on it."

"I can't leave him," I said. "I can't go without him."

"Go with me," she said, "Please, Menn, please. I have to go, we have to go. I can't be here . . . I'm . . . I'm pregnant. I have to get away from Emery."

I looked up at her with disbelief. "He just came back . . . "

"He came back six weeks ago . . . He's been lying low, waiting for Jimmy," she said. "Please we have to go now."

She reached for my arm again, and I suddenly felt nothing. A stunned numbness flowed through me, quieting the shaking. I let her pull me to my feet, move me to the sidewalk and behind the house. As soon as I was away from him, the numbness was replaced by a horrible, aching emptiness. We moved around the corner, and I looked at him, one last time, lying there in the street. So perfect. So still. My Nick.

And then, nothing.

Chapter Twelve

*M*ax takes his sister and niece back to the motel, but he cannot make himself go inside with them. Cole bounds out of the car and is in the building door before Menna has taken off her seatbelt.

"I don't know what to do, Max," she says, watching the door close behind the girl.

"I need to fix this," he says. He was silent for a while, before finally adding, "Netis is coming here." He sounds so confused and helpless.

"How are you going to do that?" she asks. He would have expected her to sound hopeful, but instead, she just sounds tired.

"I don't know," he says, "but I have to."

"Max, I know I asked for your help, but I don't know if any of us can do anything. Maybe I just needed a familiar face," she says.

"I guess that is all I'm good for anyway."

She groans, angrily. "Not exactly the time for your self-loathing. I am about to lose the only thing that has made my life OK since they murdered Nick, Max. I don't expect you to fix it, but I do expect you to focus."

He stares at her angry face. It was such a controlled censure, especially from Menna.

"I'm sorry," he says. "I will make it right."

Menna looks at him quizzically, and then steps out of the car and closes the door behind her. He sees her shoulders slump as she moves in a way too familiar to him. She is defeated.

He wanders aimlessly for an hour, checking his watch frequently, feeling Netis' impending arrival heavily. He loves her, he knows, intensely. Maybe the way Menna had loved Nick. Maybe he is capable of that. But the thought of her here, in this place where he had failed so monumentally, so often, fills him with dread.

The hill feels foreign to him, as it did when he left a few weeks after the funeral, after they officially closed the investigation. He has a memory of this place that Menna does not—of meeting Molly here that morning as she headed towards their house. She had emerged with defiance on her face. "You go, Max," she had said before she even reached him. "I am going to the police. I need to try."

He had stood then, as silent as he is now, gathering all of the resolve he could before he had uttered the words, and told her that Nick was gone. He was still haunted by the memory of watching her hear what he said, watching her turn wordlessly and head back into the trees. The memory of her screaming once she was surrounded by the woods, this time with a different kind of agony, still echoes in his head. He tries to sit there, to think, but cannot and heads back into the woods.

Finally, he finds himself at a small, overgrown pile of earth near the fence, and sits next to it.

"I remember when they buried you here," he says, hating himself a bit for saying it out loud. And then, after a long, long time he says what he means to say. "I'm sorry, Nick. I don't know how to help her."

Silence.

He shakes his head and stands, paces, and stares at the pile of earth for a while longer. He waits, wishing that somehow he would know what to do.

The sun is setting on them, and he knows that the darkness will make it nearly impossible to get back, but he cannot leave yet.

He paces, breathing loudly, cursing audibly over and over, and finally sits again, and closes his eyes to think. After a few minutes, a sense of purpose fills him. "I'll make it right," he says, and he heads out of the woods quickly and purposefully.

He reaches his car just as full dark overtakes him, and searches the glove box for what he needs. It is there, buried under piles of paper and old receipts, and slides more easily into his pocket than he would have thought it would. It thuds lazily against his hip as he heads down Maple, fairly sure that he will find Emery there.

He is right, as it turns out. As soon as he enters, he sees Emery sitting at the bar. He is hunched over, staring into a glass. Max stares at him for a moment, trying to see a trace of the man who had terrified him so intensely as a child. He sees only someone drunk, growing fat, and tired. He sees someone who hit his sister, who destroyed Menna once, and now is trying to do it again.

The bar is nearly full, so Max easily finds a seat far enough away from the man to look unassuming. Emery doesn't notice him, but sits steadily, downing one drink after another. Max orders a soda and sips it slowly as he watches, an action which is familiar to him.

A woman from his high school sits next to him. "What you doing all alone?" she asks. He feels a moment of panic that she will recognize him, but her slurred speech and glazed eyes tell him he is safe.

"I'm waiting for someone," he tells her impatiently.

"Want some company while you wait?" she asks, running two fingers up his arm.

"No," he says coldly, and she gets up and leaves, muttering a string of insults loudly enough for him to hear.

The jukebox plays song after song, few of which Max recognizes. In the bar where he met Netis, all of the music was rock anthems and late seventies classics. Here it is straight country, its twill and twang numbing him and angering him all at once. Max simply watches.

Emery stays until after midnight. Max knows that Netis has been at the motel for hours now. The frequent buzzing of the phone in his pocket signals that her annoyance and impatience has turned to worry. As he thinks of her, a look of regret passes his face. He imagines her as she was when he left, sitting so peacefully and holding on to the last minutes they had. She had known what he had not.

Emery is drinking cheap beer and making pathetic attempts at conversation with the women that move around him. They all move away from him quickly, almost desperately. Max shudders, imagining this man with Cole. His niece, so bright and buoyant, and the sense of purpose on Menna's face as she spoke of the girl, these all whirl around within him.

He feels a sense of relief as Emery stumbles out of the bar, and silently follows him into the street.

There are several people sitting out front, loudly talking. They all greet Emery, and ignore this now-stranger who emerges behind him. "Later," Emery calls over his shoulder, as he walks across Maple. When he reaches the other side, Max calls his name.

Emery turns to face him. "Ah, little brother, come here to try and defend your sister?" He is struggling to stand still enough to meet Max's gaze.

"No," Max says quietly.

"Gonna gape at me, and fall down some more?" Emery asks. His speech is slurred, and Max can smell the beer on him though he is standing a few feet away.

"No, Emery, you're not so scary anymore," he says.

Emery steps closer to him. "You feel like a big man, now? Like you could take me on?"

"I'm not going to take you on, Emery, I'm just not letting you hurt my sister any more than you already have," he says. "So you are going to walk away and leave them alone. You don't want Cole anyway."

"Don't tell me what I fucking want," Emery screams, staggering slightly as he does. "I want what is mine, and that kid is mine. Your sister can name her after some fucking Indian all she wants, but she's mine."

"What are you going to do with a kid, Emery? You gonna help her with her homework from the bar? Let it go," Max says with all the intensity he can infuse in his voice.

"Fuck you, little brother, and get away from me before I have to hurt you," Emery yells again. The people across the street have taken a greater interest in the conversation.

"I am giving you one more chance to let it go. You can hit me, you can scream at me, but you aren't taking Cole."

"That kid is mine," Emery says. "You two can't keep her from me."

Max says nothing for a long while, seeing Emery's confusion grow. Finally, he takes a step closer to him. "Emery, do you remember Nick?"

"That fucking Indian? Of course, I do," Emery says. He moves a step closer to Max.

"Yes," Max says. "The fucking Indian that you and Jimmy Reid killed."

Emery blinks heavily. The people across the street have quieted, enthralled by the confrontation they see unfolding. They had heard what Max had said, and were now listening intently.

"Jimmy killed him," Emery said. "It wasn't me."

"It might as well have been," Max says. He closes the distance between them in one quick stride. Emery's eyes widen for a second, and then narrow.

"What do you care about it? That was years ago," Emery says. His spit sprays Max, filing his nostrils with an acrid liquor smell.

"He was my friend," Max says. "You and Jimmy Reid killed my friend."

"Jimmy's dead, little brother, just like that fucking Indian. And I ain't killed nobody."

Max falls silent again, never looking away from Emery's face. "You're not taking Cole from my sister," he says firmly.

"Fuck you," Emery says, and pushes Max. He attempts to push him hard, but more falls into him.

Max takes one step back, and reaches in his pocket. "You're not taking her," he says again as he sinks the knife into Emery's side. He feels warmth rush over his hand.

Emery looks shocked and then gargles incoherently. When he steps back from Max, the people across the street see the knife protruding from him. They watch as he falls, knowing somehow by the decisive thud his body makes on the pavement that he is dead.

For a moment, the street is silent. Max stares, almost surprised, and wonders to himself if he meant it to go that far.

The shock settles, and the crowd in front of the bar begins to react. They shout in surprise and anger, and rush towards them.

Max turns quickly, moves past a few buildings with his bloody hand firmly planted in his pockets and ducks inside the deli. He mounts the steps to the motel rooms quickly and noisily, and goes straight to Menna's door. As he closes his fist to knock, he stares at the blood on his hand with confusion.

Menna opens the door, her face full of concern. "Max, what happened?" she asks immediately, and he takes a step backwards into the hallway.

"You're safe," he says.

The next door opens, and Netis steps out. "Max?" she says, looking from his hand to his face.

He turns to look at her, her dark eyes probing him for some sort of answer to a question she is unsure of. "Netis," he says. He reaches his clean, bloodless hand to her, putting it on the side of her face.

"Max what did you do?" she asks, her voice suddenly full of concern.

"I made it right," he says. "I finally made it right."

"Made what right?"

He stares at her, into the darkness of her eyes, and smiles in a small way. "Everything. You read it all, you know it all. I've ended it."

"Max?" It is now Menna moving towards him.

"I had to, Menna," he says. "I tried to talk him out of it, tried to make it go away, but he wouldn't listen."

"Max!" Netis says again. Her voice is now angry and scared. "Max, you have to tell me what you did."

"I made it right, I took care of you, Menna," he looks at his sister. "I'm just so sorry it took me so long."

Menna nods as though she now understands, and Cole appears in the door behind her.

"What's happening?" Cole asks.

Max looks at her. "Cole, take care of your aunt."

Netis puts her hand to the side of his face and pulls it towards her, makes him look at her. "Please tell me you said that because you're coming home with me. Please."

He kisses her lightly, finally realizing, in that moment, that he is capable of loving her as Nick loved his sister. He is overwhelmed by sorrow and fear as he steps away from her, feels a void develop between them, replacing one that he had finally closed.

"I love you," he says, "And I'm sorry."

Blue and red lights fill the window behind him, and he hears the door downstairs open. "You're all safe, now," he says, before heading down the stairs with his hands raised above his head.

Nick

The hill was mine for the first half of my life, until I was eleven. I would go there every day when school was out, and sit, and think. I listened to the sound the trees made in the spring breeze, and commiserated with them when the June heat stifled everything.

My home was never home. It was four walls filled with anger that caged me in. I escaped to the hill every second I could, so relieved to be away and outside and somehow free. I spent hours there, and had claimed it as my own piece of the world until that day when two raven-haired twins emerged.

I heard them coming, and closed my eyes. I wished them away but the girl, who had eyes full of defiance, insisted on sitting next to me, nudging me, and goading me. I wanted to be angry and dislike her, but something about the set of her jaw made it impossible.

He brother stood near her, always her protector, it seemed, and said little. She spoke endlessly, inviting me at once into their little world. It was much like mine, so confined and so full of sadness. Her voice, however, was hopeful, and I wondered how she managed that.

They spent the whole afternoon with me there, that first day, and I soon overcame feeling intruded upon. The sound of other voices, the sensation of being around other kids, was unfamiliar and thrilling to me.

When I moved down the hill to leave, she looked over her shoulder at me, smiling slightly. I then felt something new to me, despite my isolated existence. I felt alone, and profoundly sad to see them go.

I hoped that day that they would come back, that I could share my corner of the world with them, for a little while at least.

Shauna Kelley

Photograph by Sarah Kubel

About the Author

Shauna Kelley was born in Silver Spring, Maryland to two very young, encouraging, and idealistic parents. She has been writing stories and poems since the third grade, and wrote the initial draft of a shorter version of *Max and Menna* while in high school. She attended Goucher College, where she earned a bachelor's degree in English with a Creative Writing concentration. Previous writing credits include a regular column for *The Inditer* and several short pieces of fiction.

Kelley currently resides in Baltimore, Maryland, with a mangy, ten-year-old Jack Russell that will always be known as her puppy. Her favorite pastimes include exploring Baltimore, watching "Paranormal State" or "True Blood," and cooking decedent desserts. She reads voraciously, is an avid lover of action and horror films, and can't live without Joe's Squared pizza or Chiyo Sushi.

Shauna Kelley welcomes comments, feedback,
and questions from her readers.

Find her online:

Email: mmshaunakelley@yahoo.com

Twitter: shaunak101

Blog: mmshaunakelley.blogspot.com

Lucky Press webpage:
www.LuckyPress.com/shaunakelley.html

"Engaging Books for Thoughtful Readers"

Lucky Press, LLC is a traditional, independent publishing company located in the beautiful Appalachian foothills of Athens, Ohio. Founded in 1999, it became an LLC and published its first title in 2000. From its original aim to publish books about "characters, real or imagined, who overcome adversity or experience adventure," Lucky Press has given exposure to worthwhile authors who might have been overlooked by larger houses, and expanded into the categories of health, fiction, pets, and special needs.

www.LuckyPress.com

Join us on Facebook, YouTube, and Twitter.

Visit our blog at www.luckypress.blogspot.com

LaVergne, TN USA
27 March 2011
221792LV00004B/78/P